RUDYARD KIPLING

THE JUNGLE BOOKS

Retold by: Brett Thomas
Illustrations: Per Illum
Series editor: Paulette Møller

EASY CLASSICS

Editorial assistance:
Hanne Harboe, Aschehoug
Ulla Malmmose, Aschehoug

Cover layout: Jannie Andersen
Cover illustration: County Studio, Leicester

Printed in Denmark by
Sangill Bogtryk & offset, Holme Olstrup, 1995

RUDYARD KIPLING
(1865 - 1936)

Rudyard Joseph Kipling was born in Bombay, India when it was still part of the British Empire. He lived there with his mother and father until 1871 when they left for England. The young Kipling was left in the care of his aunt in Portsmouth for five unhappy years. His life with her and at the local military college he attended, are mentioned in detail in his later works. While he was at the college he began to write poetry and he had a book of poems published in 1881. The following year he went back to India as a journalist and his stories, drawings and poems made him very famous in England. His most popular works at this time were *Plain Tales from the Hills* (1888) and *Barrack-Room Ballads* (1892). In 1892 he married an American woman, Caroline Balestier, and they went to live in Vermont in the USA until 1896. It was here that Kipling wrote *The Jungle Book* (1894). Later he wrote *Kim* (1901) and the *Just So Stories* (1902). He wrote a large variety of material but the story of *Kim* is widely considered to be his best full-length novel.

In 1902 Kipling moved back to England but travelled as a reporter to South Africa where the British were fighting in the Boer War. Some of his views were considered violent and imperialistic, though, and his popularity began to decline. Despite his wealth he was never accepted by the other writers of his day. Following the outbreak of the First World War, Kipling became more sombre and serious (his only son died in 1916) but continued to produce excellent work like *A Diversity of Creatures* (1917), *Credits and Debits* (1926) and *Limits and Renewals* (1932).

Kipling refused to accept prizes awarded to him by the government but became the first English writer to receive the Nobel Prize for Literature, in 1907.

wolf

jackal (Tabaqui)

cubs

MOWGLI'S BROTHERS

It was evening in the *Seeonee hills* when Father Wolf woke up and *stretched* his *paws* to get the sleepy feeling out of them. Mother Wolf was awake and feeding her four hungry *cubs*. He looked at the moon shining through the mouth the cave and said, "Aaaargh! Time to hunt again." But before he reached the cave entrance he heard a horrible little voice say, "Good luck, King of the Wolves. And to your fine children. I hope they never forget the poor and hungry in this world."

It was Tabaqui, the *jackal*. The wolves of India hate Tabaqui because he is a thief and a liar but they are also afraid of him. Sometimes he went mad and ran through the forest attacking the other animals. Even the tigers ran from him on those days.

"Come in and look, then," said Father Wolf, "but there is nothing here to eat."

"Not for a wolf, perhaps, but a dry bone is a feast for a jackal like me," said Tabaqui and ran to the inside of the cave.

"Delicious!" said the jackal, biting on an old bone. "What beautiful children you have. Of course, in this they are like their parents."

Everybody knows that you should never *compliment* children when they can hear you and Tabaqui knew

---

Seeonee hills, an area in Central India
stretched, extended
paws, the "feet" of an animal
cubs, here, young wolves
jackal, animal like a dog, that eats what others leave
compliment, to say nice things about something or someone

this very well, too. That is why he smiled when he saw how uncomfortable Mother and Father Wolf looked now.

"Shere Khan, the Big One, is coming this way to
5 *hunt*, or so he tells me," continued Tabaqui with a little smile.

Shere Khan was the big tiger that lived thirty kilometres up the river.

"He has no *right* to do that. The Law of the Jungle
10 says he must tell us first. He will *frighten* everyone away and leave me and my family without food."

"That is why his mother called him the *Lame* One. Since he was born he has only hunted cows from the villages. Now he comes to make **our** villagers angry.
15 They will burn the grass and the trees to frighten him away and then we will have to leave, too. Thank Shere Khan for that!"

"Listen! I think I can hear him now in the valley. Why not thank him yourself?" asked Tabaqui.
20 "Get out of my cave, now!" shouted Father Wolf. "And go back to your friend and master!"

Father Wolf listened and heard the angry, noisy *growling* of a tiger that has not caught anything.

"Stupid tiger!" said the wolf. "Making so much
25 noise. Does he think our *deer* are slow and fat like his cows?"

"But listen. He is not hunting for cows or deer tonight. He is hunting for Man," said Mother Wolf.

hunt, to kill animals for food
right, here, authority
frighten, to make someone afraid
lame, having an injured leg
growl, the noise a large cat makes

6

The Law of the Jungle says that no animal must hunt for Man except to show his children how to kill. You never kill Man in your own hunting territory. Every animal knows that if you kill Man, hundreds more men will come with elephants, guns, drums and torches. Then every animal in the jungle suffers. In any case Man is a weak and defenceless creature and to kill one is not good sport.

Father Wolf could hear the loud *roars* of Shere Khan in the valley below. It was clear that the tiger had attacked but missed. Father and Mother Wolf listened again and this time heard a different sound - of something moving towards the cave. Father Wolf hid and waited to attack. When he saw some leaves move he jumped high into the air but suddenly stopped in mid-air and *landed* in the same place again.

"Man!" he shouted. "A man-cub! Look!"

In front of them was a very small brown baby boy holding the branch of a small tree. He looked up at Father Wolf and laughed. Father Wolf picked the baby up and carried it carefully between its teeth into the cave.

deer

tiger (Shere Khan)

roar, the noise a tiger or lion makes
land, here, come to the floor

7

"How small and soft! And how *naked*, too!" Mother Wolf had never seen a man-cub before. As Father Wolf put the boy down, he moved next to Mother Wolf and her cubs. Once there, he began to eat with the others.

5   Then, as they watched him, the light of the moon was suddenly blocked by a large figure in the mouth of the cave. It was Shere Khan. And behind him was Tabaqui.

"Well, well. The great Shere Khan. And what can
10 we do for you?" said Father Wolf with anger in his eyes.

"Give me my man-cub. His parents ran away and he came in here. He's mine."

But Shere Khan was a big tiger and the mouth of the cave too small for him to get through.

15 "The Wolves are free and only take orders from the Head of the *Pack*, not from a sheep-killer. The man-cub is ours to kill if we want."

"If you want! You are talking to Shere Khan, you cave-dog!"

20 Mother Wolf jumped away from the cubs and looked at the tiger with fire in her eyes.

"And **I** am Raksha and this man-cub is mine! **Mine**, do you hear? And he will not be killed. He will live with me and grow to run with the Pack. And one day
25 he will hunt **you**, killer of man-cubs! So take your broken leg and go back to your mother. Go!"

Shere Khan knew that it was not a good idea to fight with Raksha and slowly walked away.

"You will see how he is mine in the end, family of
30 thieves," he said as he left.

naked, here, without hair
pack, here, a group of wolves

"Do you really think the Pack will let us keep him, Mother?" asked Father Wolf.

"They must. He is already one of the family. Look how he eats with the cubs. He is like a little frog. That is what I will call him - Mowgli, as we call the frogs. One day you will hunt Shere Khan and kill him, little Mowgli."

Father Wolf was a little worried. The Law of the Jungle says that when cubs can walk they must be presented to the rest of the Pack. The cubs are free to go where they like until they kill their first deer. During this time no other wolf may hurt the cubs.

9

As soon as the cubs could walk, Father Wolf took them with Mowgli and Mother Wolf to the rock where the wolves had their meetings. There were more than forty wolves sitting on the rock. Above them all sat
5 Akela, the great grey wolf who, with his strength and intelligence, was leader of the Pack. Below him sat the other older wolves and, lower down, the three-year-olds. These were very aggressive and dreamt of the day they would fight to become leader of the pack.

10 The wolf-parents pushed their young into the light where the older wolves could see them better. "Look well, wolves!" cried Akela from above as all the cubs from the Pack played in the circle of light. Then it was Mowgli's turn. Nervously, Mother Wolf pushed the
15 man-cub towards the other cubs. "Look well, wolves!" she heard again. Akela showed no surprise. He was not young and had seen many man-cubs in his time. But then, from the trees behind the rocks, the wolves heard the angry roar of Shere Khan,

20 "He is mine. Give the man-cub to me! The Free People have no need for him. What can the Pack do with a man-cub?"

"The Pack does not need others to make its decisions. What are the feelings of the Wolf Brothers?"
25 replied Akela.

One of the younger wolves growled, "Shere Khan is right. What are we to do with a man-cub?"

When there is a problem of this type in the Jungle, the Law offers a solution: If two members of the Pack
30 *speak for* the cub, other than his mother and father, he is free to enter the Pack.

| *speak for*, to speak in defence of somebody

10

"Will anyone speak for this cub?" asked Akela but nobody replied. Mother Wolf was preparing herself for the last fight of her life if it were necessary.

Then a big figure with a soft, sleepy voice stood up.

"**I** speak for the man-cub." It was old Baloo, the ⁵

brown bear. As he was the teacher of the young wolves, he was the only other animal who could speak at these meetings. "He cannot hurt anyone and I will teach him myself," he continued.

5   "That is one," said Akela, "but you need one more. Will anyone else speak for this cub?"

There was a moment of silence and then an enormous shadow fell across the circle of moonlight. Bagheera, the Black Panther, was respected by all jungle animals. He was clever, strong and very dangerous. And he had a voice like wild honey.

"Akela and you, the Free People. Of course I have no right to speak at your meetings, but I understand that our Law says you can buy the life of a cub, for a price, and that anyone can pay that price. Is that correct?"

The young wolves, who were always hungry, cried up to Akela,

"Let Bagheera speak. He can pay the price!" So Akela let Bagheera continue.

20   "A naked man-cub is a poor meal. It is better to let him grow. Baloo has spoken for him and I will offer a fat, fresh bull that I killed this afternoon as my price for the cub."

The idea of a big fat bull was too much for the wolves, who decided to let Mowgli join the Pack.

"Look well, wolves," said Akela again. This time the wolves looked carefully at the man-cub before they ran off to find the bull that Bagheera promised them. Akela, Bagheera, Baloo and Mowgli's new family waited behind and heard Shere Khan roaring his anger in the distance.

"Roar well, tiger," said Bagheera, "for one day the man-cub will stop your roaring, if I know men."

12

"It was a good thing to take the man-cub," said Akela. "Men are very wise and maybe one day he will be a help for us. Now you must train him in the ways of the Free People," he said, looking at Father Wolf.

And that is how Mowgli entered the Seeonee wolf-pack, with Baloo's word and Bagheera's bull. 5

bear (Baloo)

black panther (Bagheera)

KAA'S HUNTING

This story takes place before the Seeonee wolf-pack sent Mowgli away and before his fight with Shere Khan, the tiger. Mowgli was studying the Law of the Jungle with Baloo. The bear Baloo was very happy to
5 have Mowgli as his student. He was not like the wolf-cubs, who learned only what they needed to know as wolves. Mowgli was a man-cub and needed more than the Hunting Song of the wolves. For that reason Baloo, a very serious teacher, was able to teach him all
10 he knew about the Law. Because Mowgli could climb, Baloo taught him the Wood Laws, and because he could swim the man-cub learned the Water Laws. So Mowgli knew how to see a bad branch in a tree, how to speak kindly to *bees* and *bats* and *water-snakes*. He also
15 needed to know the Strangers' Hunting Call. This was a very important call in the jungle. You use it every time you go hunting outside your usual hunting territory. The call is: "I am hungry. Let me hunt for food here"; and the answer you must wait for is: "You can
20 hunt for food, but not for *pleasure*."

bat

bee

water-snake

pleasure, fun, enjoyment

Mowgli needed to learn these and many other Laws by heart. Sometimes he was tired after repeating the same thing a hundred times and Baloo hit him on the head to keep his attention. Sometimes Bagheera, the Black Panther came to watch the class and see how 5 Mowgli, his personal favourite, was getting on with his studies. He did not like to see Baloo hitting the boy. The Bear told Bagheera, "A man's cub is a man's cub and needs to know **all** the Laws of the Jungle."

"But you see how small he is," said the Panther, who 10 was always kind to Mowgli. "Do you think he can remember so much?"

"Nothing in the jungle is too small to learn or too small to die. That's why I teach him these things, and I only hit him, and very softly, when he forgets." 15

"Softly! Look at the marks on his face from your softness," said Bagheera.

"Better to have the marks from me, who loves him, than be killed by *ignorance*," Baloo replied in his usual serious manner. "Today he is learning the Master 20 Words that will protect him from birds, the Snake-People and other hunters from outside his pack. A little *tap* on the head for all that protection is fair, don't you think?"

"Well, be careful not to kill him with your tapping. 25 But what Master Words are you talking about?" Bagheera began to admire his long, blue *claws*, "As you know, I never use them myself as I rarely need to ask for help but still .... "

"Mowgli can tell you himself. Come, Little Brother." 30

ignorance, not knowing
tap, a small, light hit
claws, animal fingernails

15

"My head hurts," said Mowgli, climbing down from a tree. "I came to speak to my friend, Bagheera, not **you**, fat old Baloo."

"*It's all the same to me*," replied Baloo, a little hurt by Mowgli's words. "Tell Bagheera the new Master Words you have learned today."

"For which people - I know them all," said Mowgli.

"For the Hunting-People then, as you are so clever."

"We are of one blood, you and I," said Mowgli with a bear accent.

"Good. Now the birds."

Mowgli repeated the same words with the whistle of a *kite* and then with the hiss of the snake for the Snake-People.

"Well, there you are," said Baloo with *pride*. "Now he need not be afraid of anyone."

"Except perhaps his own people," thought Bagheera to himself with sadness.

"Soon I will have my own tribe to lead through the branches," Mowgli shouted from on top of Bagheera's back.

monkey

kite

it's all the same to me, I don't care what you say
kite, a large bird like a hawk or an eagle
pride, here, feeling happy with himself

16

"What in the name of the Jungle are you talking about now, dreamer?" asked the Panther.

"Yes, and we will throw branches and dirt down at old Baloo," Mowgli continued.

In two seconds, Baloo pulled Mowgli from Bagheera's back and threw him to the floor, holding him there between his two front paws. The boy knew that the Bear was very angry.

"You have been with the Bandar-log - the Monkey-People. That is very, very sad, little man-cub," said Baloo as Mowgli looked to Bagheera for help. But Bagheera's eyes were as hard as stone.

"You hurt my head and the grey monkeys felt *pity* for me," cried Mowgli.

"The pity of the Monkey-People is like snow in a hot summer!" shouted Baloo.

"They gave me fruits and nuts to eat and said I was like them without the tail. They said that I was going to be their leader one day."

"They have no leaders," said Bagheera. "They always *lie*."

"Why can I not go with the Monkey-People? They are like me. They stand on two legs, they don't hit me, they play all day. Let me go and play with them, Baloo!"

"Listen, man-cub," said the Bear, with his most serious voice. "I have taught you the Laws of all the people of the jungle. Except the Monkey-People. They have no law and no respect for the laws of the other jungle peoples. They listen and copy what they see but they

pity, sympathy for someone with problems
lie, to never tell the truth

have no good ideas of their own. They have no leaders
and no memory but sit around *chattering* all day about
how clever they are. They are not a serious people and
we want nothing from them. We do not drink where
5 they drink, go where they go, or hunt where they hunt.
Do you ever hear us talk of the Monkey-People, man-
cub?"

chatter, talk a lot about stupid things

"No," whispered Mowgli. The jungle was completely silent now.

"The Jungle-People don't talk or think about them. They are *shameless* and dirty and their only wish, if they have a wish at all, is to be *noticed* by the Jungle-People." 5

As Baloo spoke a shower of dirt, nuts and branches fell on his head and there was much *hysterical* laughter coming from the trees above him.

"The Monkey-People are no friends of ours, it is true, but Baloo was wrong not to tell you about them," said 10 Bagheera under a fresh shower of dirt.

Everything Baloo said was true. The monkeys lived in the trees and other animals rarely looked up in their direction so there was little contact. But they were quick to scream *ridiculous* songs, to throw sticks at sick 15 animals and to *provoke* the other animals into a fight in the trees. But the other animals tried not to notice them. That is why the monkeys were so happy when Mowgli spoke to them and that Baloo was talking about them for the first time. One of them had a bril- 20 liant idea - Mowgli could make *shelters* for them from pieces of wood and branches. The monkeys were going to catch him and force him to teach them how to do it. Then everybody in the jungle was going to see how clever the Monkey-People were, and were going to 25 want to be as intelligent as they were. That was their idea and that was why they followed Baloo, Bagheera

shameless, immodest and uncaring
notice, see or hear
hysterical, mad and uncontrolled
ridiculous, funny
provoke, here, to anger and irritate
shelter, cover to protect someone from the rain

and Mowgli through the forest. They waited in the trees for the three to have their afternoon sleep. Mowgli lay between his friends and, as his eyes closed, decided never to speak to the monkeys again. Mowgli
5 did not sleep for long. He woke to find himself in the arms of two monkeys who carried him up into the trees, away from Bagheera who ran up the trees after them, showing his white teeth. But the big Panther was too heavy for the small branches at the top and the
10 monkeys easily escaped. This made the monkeys even happier. Now Bagheera was noticing them, too. They really were a very clever people.

As the monkeys carried him through the high branches, Mowgli sometimes saw over the tops of the
15 trees into the distance. Although he was feeling a little sick from so many ups-and-downs, the experience was not too horrible. But after a while he began to get angry with the monkeys. He wanted to be with Baloo and Bagheera again but now they were far away and out of
20 sight. He looked around for help. Below him there were only trees and more trees. Above him in the clear, blue sky and far away he saw a hunting-bird looking for food. From this great distance, Chil the Kite was watching the Bandar-log and saw they were carrying
25 something. He was hungry and was hoping that the monkeys would drop their prisoner, as they often did. He was surprised to hear the Kite-call, "We are of one blood, you and I."

The Kite flew closer to see the little brown face that
30 called to him.

Mowgli shouted, "Follow me and tell Baloo the Bear and Bagheera the Panther where the Bandar-log take me. I am Mowgli, of the Seeonee Pack. They call me

the Man-cub."

As the boy disappeared into the branches with the monkeys, Chil flew high into the sky and followed the Monkey-People with his telescopic eyes.

5   Far below him, Bagheera and Baloo were both angry and sad as they ran through the jungle after the monkeys.

"You were very *unwise* not to tell the man-cub about the Bandar-log," shouted Bagheera as he ran. "All that
10 hitting him on the head was for nothing in the end. Bah! This is stupid. We will never catch them at this speed. Let's stop for a moment. We need a plan." They sat and considered the situation carefully. It was truly going to be difficult. No other creatures were as fast as
15 the monkeys in the trees. They hoped that Mowgli remembered the Master Words. He knew them well before when Bagheera asked him before. Just as they were beginning to lose hope, Baloo suddenly stood up and shouted, "Oh, why did I not think of it before? It
20 is as Hathi the Wild Elephant says: "Everyone has his enemy"; and the Monkey-People are no different, for their enemy is Kaa the Rock *Python*. They are afraid of him with good reason, for Kaa can climb as well as they can and steals their young when they sleep. Let's go and
25 find Kaa."

Bagheera was not so sure. The python was not of their tribe and had evil eyes. Bagheera knew that the monkeys hated Kaa, though, so they decided to look for him. They hoped he was hungry. When they found him
30 he was wearing his new skin. Like all snakes, Kaa

unwise, not clever
python, a very large snake that crushes its enemies to death

changed his skin from time to time. He lay in the sun, *licking* his lips. That was a good sign. He was hungry. Bagheera and Baloo were very careful now. A snake with a new skin is a little blind at first and could attack an unexpected visitor. 5

"Good hunting!" shouted Baloo. All pythons have very poor hearing. The three told stories of their past hunts and battles. They agreed that things had been better when they were younger - they were all getting older now. Then Kaa told them of his last battle with 10 the Bandar-log and how he had fallen from a tree as he was close to attacking them.

"Those stupid creatures began to call me horrible names," said Kaa.

"Yes. I heard they said you were a footless, yellow 15 *worm*," said Bagheera, looking at Baloo.

"Did they say **that**?" asked Kaa and licked his lips again.

"That or something similar," said Bagheera, looking down at his claws. "But you know these monkeys. They 20 always shout things at us but we never listen to them. They did say you had no teeth, though, and could no longer kill the smallest of goats. Very silly creatures, the Bandar-log."

An old snake like Kaa rarely showed his feelings but 25 Bagheera and Baloo could see he was angry now.

"I heard them moving through the trees this afternoon," said Kaa. "They seemed happy."

Then Bagheera told Kaa that they were following the Monkey-People who had stolen the man-cub. Kaa 30

lick, make wet with a tongue
worm, small, usually pink creature with no legs that lives in earth

23

knew of this creature that ran with the wolves. There were lots of stories in the jungle. Kaa did not believe them. Baloo told him the stories of the man-cub were true and told Kaa how much they all loved him.

5 "And that is why we come to you, great Kaa. We know how much the monkeys fear you."

"Yes, so they should. A yellow worm, eh? Which way did they go?"

At that point Chil the Kite flew down close to 10 them.

"I have seen your Mowgli, the man-cub of the Seeonee. The Bandar-log have taken him to the monkey city, to the Cold Place. I told the bats there to watch closely. You never know when those monkeys will 15 leave. Your man-cub is very clever. He knew the Master Words," said Chil before flying away for the night.

The Cold Place was a *deserted* city in the middle of the jungle where the Jungle-People never went. Kaa and Bagheera decided to hurry there ahead of Baloo, 20 who moved more slowly.

In the Cold Place, the monkeys were very pleased with themselves for bringing the man-cub to this Lost City. It was a new experience for Mowgli. Most of the buildings were now ruins, overgrown with trees and 25 plants, but this Indian city seemed very beautiful to him. There were *marble* fountains, palaces and temples, all of them in ruins. You could see where the streets once were and where the elephants had lived before. The monkeys did not know what to do with the city, 30 though they knew the other animals were *envious* of

deserted, abandoned, nobody lived there
marble, hard and expensive stone often used for making floors
envious, wanting something they do not have

24

their city and, of course, their intelligence. They ran around, fighting and screaming or getting lost in the underground passages but they had no idea what they were doing or why they were doing it. Mowgli did not
5 really understand them, either. One monkey made a speech about their bright future and asked Mowgli to show the monkeys how to make shelters against the rain. Mowgli began to tie some sticks together but the monkeys found it too difficult, decided it was boring
10 and began hitting each other. Mowgli was getting hungry. He looked around for food. He tried the Strangers' Hunting Call but there were no Jungle-People around. "How foolish and boring these Bandar-log are," he thought to himself. He tried to escape behind the city
15 wall but the monkeys took him back. Mowgli thought how funny it was that such stupid creatures could live in this ruined but beautiful city. He looked up to the moon and saw a black cloud coming closer to it. "Do these people never sleep?" he asked himself.

20 Bagheera and Kaa were watching the same cloud from behind the city wall. They needed help against so many monkeys and were waiting for the cloud to cover the moon. Kaa moved to the hill behind the palace so that he could move faster. Then the cloud covered
25 the moon completely. Mowgli heard soft footsteps and knew that Bagheera was there. He heard Bagheera attacking the hundreds of monkeys that separated him from Mowgli. "Attack! Kill! There is only one!" cried one of them, and Bagheera was covered by a *mass* of
30 grey monkeys pulling at his tail and fur. Another group took Mowgli and threw him down through the roof of

| *mass*, here, a very large group

a small building. It was 5 or 6 metres from the floor to
the roof but Mowgli landed on his feet. Then he heard
things moving in the dark.

"We are of one blood, you and I," said Mowgli, using
the Snake's Call.   5

"Well, be careful where you put your feet then, Little Brother," said one of the cobras.

Outside, Bagheera was fighting for his life. "To the
water-tank, Bagheera. They will not go into the water,"
shouted Mowgli. The Black Panther slowly pulled him-   10
self into the water-tank and away from all the monkeys,
who he left behind him jumping up and down outside.
Then he heard Baloo arrive and the noise of his paws
sending monkeys into the air. There were so many
monkeys that Bagheera could not climb out of the   15
water to help his friend. Where was Kaa? Bagheera
could wait no longer and, using the Snake's Call, cried

out, "We are of one blood, you and I!" Then he heard it. Kaa came flying down the hill using his head and long hard body like a very large metal hammer to send the monkeys in all directions. His first attack was on
5 the crowd of monkeys around Baloo. The monkeys were *terrified* and ran away, screaming, "Kaa! It is Kaa! Run! Run!"

Every monkey in the jungle feared Kaa and knew how he silently climbed trees and carried away the
10 strongest monkey he could find. No monkey had lived after a *hug* from Kaa and no monkey could look into Kaa's eyes. They ran and jumped onto the walls and trees of the Lost City in terror. Then Kaa opened his mouth and spoke one long hiss. The monkeys were
15 silent and did not move. Bagheera said he would get the man-cub before the monkeys attacked again.

"They will not attack. They will not move until I say ssssso," hissed Kaa. "Did I hear you call for help, Bagheera? I was not sure with so much noise."

20 "I, er, I did cry out in the battle once, yes," said Bagheera.

Kaa used his hard head to break the wall of the

a hug from Kaa

terrified, very afraid
hug, an embrace or, here, a squeeze

28

building where Mowgli stood with the cobras. "Stand back from the wall, Poison-People," he told the snakes and broke a hole big enough for Mowgli to climb through. He ran out and put his little arms around the big necks of Baloo and Bagheera.

"Oh, look! Blood! They have hurt you, my Brothers!" said the man-cub.

"Yes, but now we have you, little frog, so everything is all right," said Baloo with a smile.

"Not everything," said Bagheera. "But we will talk about that later. First you must give your thanks to Kaa. He saved your life."

"We are of one blood, you and I," said Mowgli, "and from today and for ever, what is mine will be yours, and what I eat you can eat also if you are hungry."

"So this is the man-cub," said Kaa. "Thank you for your fine words, Little One. But be careful not to cross me when I have new skin, for you are much like a Bandar-log. Now you should leave with your friends."

Then Kaa returned to where the Bandar-log waited in silence. He began a strange dance, moving around in circles very slowly and singing softly. He called the monkeys closer and Mowgli had to stop Bagheera and Baloo from walking towards Kaa. They, like the monkeys, were hypnotised. The two friends looked at Mowgli and woke from their dreaming. Mowgli could only see a big snake making strange movements and did not understand why his friends were so happy when he woke them.

"Come! We must leave. This Kaa is too strong for me and I do not think we should see what happens next. He will not be hungry tomorrow, of that we can be sure," said Baloo.

"Mowgli!" said Bagheera, looking Mowgli in the eye. "You have caused many problems today. We have lost much hunting-time, much hair and much blood, but worse than that, I, Bagheera, the Black Panther, had to call to Kaa for help. Then we were both made to look foolish by his dancing. All of this has a price and you have to pay it. It is Jungle Law."

"You are right to *punish* me," said Mowgli. "I have been very foolish and will never be so foolish again."

"You are right, Bagheera. He must be punished. But remember, he is only a little man-cub," said Baloo.

Bagheera hit Mowgli five or six times - very light hits for a big panther - and Mowgli cried in silence. Baloo and Bagheera waited for the boy to finish his crying. Then Baloo picked Mowgli up and sat him on Bagheera's long back.

"Come, Little Brother, it is time to take you home."

punish, to make somebody suffer for their wrong actions

MOWGLI'S BROTHERS (II)

It was ten years now since Mowgli first walked into the cave and found his new family. In that time he had many adventures as he grew up with the wolves. They of course were fully grown a long time before he was, so
5 he learned how to live in the jungle with Father Wolf's help at first. He learned to understand the movements of the grass, the smells in the night air and the singing of the bats and *owls* above his head. When he was not learning he was sleeping or washing in the forest pools,
10 or sometimes eating honey with Baloo. He sat with the wolves at Council Rock and soon learned that they always looked away if he *stared* at any of them. Sometimes he helped the wolves to keep their coats clean or to take *thorns* from their paws.

15 At other times he went to watch people from the village working in their fields. He never went close to them, though, not since the day Bagheera showed him a *trap* the villagers had made. He liked spending time

owl

thorn in paw

trap

stare, look at without closing your eyes
trap, for catching wild animals

with Bagheera who hunted at night and slept in the day. Mowgli learned to kill like Bagheera but the Black Panther told him he must never kill bulls or cows because that was the price Bagheera paid for Mowgli at Council Rock. That was the Law of the Jungle. 5

Mother Wolf told him to always be careful with Shere Khan but as he was a young boy he never really listened. Shere Khan was always meeting Mowgli in the jungle. He was now a good friend of some of the younger wolves who ate what he left them after his 10 hunts. Akela did not agree to this but he was getting old now. Shere Khan sometimes attacked the young wolves for letting themselves be led by a young man-cub and a dying wolf, "They say you cannot look him in the eyes," he said. The wolves just growled and 15 looked away.

Bagheera knew about this because his eyes and ears were everywhere. He told Mowgli that Shere Khan was going to kill him one day but the boy just laughed, "I have the Pack and you and old Baloo. Why must I be 20 afraid?"

"We have told you many times to be careful. I have told you, Baloo has told you and even Tabaqui the Jackal has told you," said the Black Panther.

"Tabaqui?" laughed the boy. "Last time I saw him he 25 told me that I was a man's cub and that I was only good at eating peanuts from the floor. I picked him up and threw him against a tree."

"That was not clever," continued Bagheera seriously. "I know he is a trouble-maker but he can tell you many 30 things you need to know. Shere Khan will not kill you here in the jungle. But when Akela and the other old-er wolves die, the young wolves will say, as Shere Khan has told them, that there is no place in the Pack for a man-cub."

"But they are my brothers!" said Mowgli. "I was born with them, I have played, hunted and eaten with them.
5   I have followed the Law of the Jungle. Why do they not want me in the Pack?"

Bagheera looked at Mowgli and half-closed his eyes. "Look here, under my chin, Little Brother," he said. "Nobody in the jungle knows this. That place where
10 there is no fur is because I was chained in the King's Palace. I was also, like you, born among men and escaped when I was big enough, tired of being a toy for them. I learned their ways, which is why I am more terrible in the jungle than Shere Khan."

15 "It's true. All the jungle is afraid of Bagheera, except Mowgli," said the boy.

"But you are a man's cub," said the Panther gently, "and you will return to your people one day. Man always returns to his brothers in the end and so will
20 you. If the Pack doesn't kill you first."

"But why do they want to kill me?" asked Mowgli.

"Look at me," Bagheera replied seriously. "Look me in the eyes."

Mowgli turned and looked Bagheera in the eye. Two
25 seconds later, the Black Panther looked down.

"That is why, Little Brother," he said. "I lived with men but even I cannot look you in the eye. That's why they want to kill you - because they are afraid of you."

"I did not know these things before," said Mowgli.

30 "You must be careful now," said Bagheera. "I think the next time old Akela *misses his kill*, the Pack will be

---

| *miss his kill*, attack an animal but not be able to kill it.

34

against him and you, and then - wait! I know what you must do. Bring the Red Flower!" he said, jumping to his feet. "Quickly, run down to the village and take some of the Red Flower that they grow there. That will be a stronger friend to you than Baloo, Bagheera or your friends in the Pack. Quick, go now!"

Every animal in the jungle is afraid of fire and cannot even say its real name. They call it Red Flower when they talk about it.

"I will go now," said Mowgli, putting his arm around Bagheera's neck, "but are you sure Shere Khan is behind this?"

"I'm as sure as it is possible to be," said the Black Panther.

"Then I will pay him back for it, more than he *bargains for*," said Mowgli.

"That is man talking," said Bagheera to himself as he lay down again.

Mowgli ran back to the cave to tell Mother Wolf that he was leaving for the village that evening. She could see that he was not happy but Mowgli left before she could ask him what the problem was.

On his way down over the hills he stopped suddenly. Behind him he could hear the Pack attacking a male deer. He heard the young wolves calling to Akela to attack and also the old wolf missing his kill. He started to run again, faster than before, down to the village.

"Bagheera was right," he told himself. "Tomorrow is an important day for Akela and for me."

Now in the village, he stood outside a house and watched the fire burning inside. A woman threw some

bargain for, expect

black rocks onto it. "They are much like me," he thought to himself. When the house was empty next morning he took some of the hot red rocks and put them inside a pot. He threw in some pieces of wood as he had seen the woman doing and ran up the hill where he saw Bagheera.

"Akela missed last night," he said. "They were going to kill him last night but they wanted you, too. They are looking for you now. Are you not afraid of the Red Flower, then?"

"Afraid? No, I remember sleeping next to it before I was a wolf. It was warm," Mowgli replied.

Mowgli took the Red Flower back to his cave and

made sure there was always enough wood to keep it burning. When, in the evening, Tabaqui came to tell Mowgli that the Pack was waiting for him at the Rock, Mowgli stood up and laughed all the way to the Rock, taking his Red Flower with him.

When he arrived he saw that Akela was no longer sitting on the Pack Leader's rock. It was now empty. Mowgli sat at a distance with Bagheera and hid the fire from view. Shere Khan was talking loudly without asking Akela for permission. He had never done this before.

Mowgli jumped to his feet. "What is this, Free People?" he shouted, "Is Shere Khan now Leader of the Pack? Who has told this dog's son to be our leader?"

There was a lot of shouting between the wolves, some of them for and others against Mowgli. Finally an older wolf told them to be quiet. "Let the Dead Wolf speak!" he shouted. When a wolf misses its kill, it is called the Dead Wolf because the others will soon kill it.

"Wolves, I have led you for many years and last night some of you laid a trap for me and I missed my kill. You have the right to kill me and I only ask for one thing. You should attack me one at a time - that is my right as Leader of the Pack, by the Law of the Jungle."

Shere Khan saw that none of the wolves was prepared to fight Akela alone and finally said, "Who cares what this old toothless fool has to say? It is the man-cub who has lived too long. Give him to me or I will hunt here always and not leave one bone for you."

Half of the Pack shouted, "Let him go! Send the man-cub back to his people. There is no place for him here. Man!"

"No!" shouted the tiger, "Then he will make the villagers attack us. Give him to me, he is mine."

Akela lifted his old head, "He has done nothing wrong. He eats with us and follows the Law of the Jungle."

"And I paid a bull for him," said Bagheera softly. "I will certainly fight for that, if it is necessary."

"He is a man and has no place in the jungle," continued Shere Khan. "Give him to me!"

"He is our brother and some of you want to kill him here!" cried Akela angrily. "I have heard how some of you now go with Shere Khan and steal children from the villages at night so I know that I speak to *cowards*. If you let the man-cub free I promise I will not fight when you come to kill me."

Many of the young wolves moved over to stand next to Shere Khan. "He is a man, a man!" they shouted.

"There is nothing more we can do now except fight, Little Brother," said Bagheera. "Now it is in your hands."

Mowgli stood up with the fire-pot in his left hand and laughed. But he was angry and sad. He had not known that the wolves hated him so much.

"Enough of this useless chatter. I am bored with it all," he said. "You have told me that I am a man so many times tonight that I no longer think of you as my brothers. No! You are just dogs now and like all dogs you will do what a man tells you to do. I have brought you some of the Red Flower that makes you all so afraid."

Mowgli threw the fire-pot onto some dry grass and

cowards, the opposite of heroes

saw the whole Council jump back from the *leaping* flames. He put a dry stick into the fire and held it above his head, making moving shadows in the dark night.

"Good!" he shouted. "Now I see that you are dogs. I
5 am leaving to go back to my people, if they are my people. But I will not be like you. I will always remember that you were my brothers and will never *betray* you in the way that you have gone against me. But there is one of you I do have to pay back."

10 Mowgli walked over to where Shere Khan sat looking stupidly at the flames and pulled him by his chin. Bagheera followed, in case of accidents.

"Up, dog!" shouted Mowgli. "Up! Or I will burn you alive. If you make one move, sheep-killer, I will stick
15 this Red Flower down your neck." Mowgli touched the tiger's side with the fire and Shere Khan ran away in fear. "Remember this, the rest of you. I am leaving now but when I come back, as a man, I will bring Shere Khan's skin on my head. And nobody here will touch
20 Akela because I say so. And now the sight of you dogs makes me feel sick. Go! Away with you!" Mowgli kicked the burning grass at the wolves who ran away howling in fear.

Nearly all the wolves left except Akela and ten oth-
25 ers who were on Mowgli's side. Mowgli looked around slowly at Bagheera and the wolves, dropped his stick on the floor and began to feel very uncomfortable. For the first time in his life, he began to cry.

"What is happening to me, Bagheera? I don't want
30 to leave the jungle and now I feel so bad. Am I dying?"

leap, jump
betray, turn against someone who trusts you

40

"No, Little Brother," said Bagheera. "They are tears of man. Now you are a man and no longer a man-cub. Let the tears fall."

Mowgli sat and cried for a long time and felt that his heart was going to break. He walked over to his cave to say goodbye to his mother, Father Wolf and the four cubs.

"You must never forget me," he said looking back at the howling wolves.

"We won't forget you, brother," said the cubs. "We will come and watch you with the man-pack and play with you at night in the fields."

"Come back soon," said Father Wolf. "Your mother and I are getting old now. Come soon."

"Come soon, son of man," said Mother Wolf. "I loved you as much as I ever loved my cubs, you know."

"I'll be back. And when I come, I will bring Shere Khan's head and skin to cover Council Rock," said Mowgli.

It was nearly morning when Mowgli walked slowly down the hill to meet those strange creatures called men.

RIKKI-TIKKI-TAVI

This is the story of the battle that Rikki-tikki-tavi fought in the bathrooms of a *bungalow* in *Segowlee*. He had some help from Dharzee, the *tailor-bird* and from Chuchundra, the timid *musk-rat* but it was really Rik-
5 ki-tikki who did the fighting.

Rikki-tikki was a *mongoose* and looked like a nervous and *furry*, little cat with a pink nose and eyes, and a tail that was a little like a brush.

Young Rikki-tikki was taken from his parents when
10 the river *flooded* his home and carried him away, leaving him almost dead in the garden of the bungalow in Segowlee. When he woke up, not knowing where he was, he heard a young boy saying: "Look, Mum! It's a dead mongoose. Shall we have a funeral for him?"

15 "Perhaps he is not dead," his mother said. "We will dry him first and see if he is alive."

When they took him into the house, the boy's father told them that the mongoose was not dead but was very tired and full of water. Rikki-tikki soon woke up and
20 immediately began to explore his new house, as a good mongoose always does. First of all, he decided to have a look at the small boy. He jumped up on the boy's shoulder and put his nose under his shirt.

"Don't be afraid, Teddy," said his father, "he wants to
25 be your friend."

> *bungalow*, a house with only one floor
> *Segowlee*, an invented name of a village in India
> *tailor-bird*, a bird in Asia that makes sophisticated nests
> *musk-rat*, a water-rat that has a smell like perfume
> *mongoose*, a small animal, like a rabbit, that kills snakes
> *furry*, with a lot of hair
> *flooded*, filled with water

42

"Is he so *tame* because we are kind to him?" asked Teddy's mother.

"All mongooses are like that," her husband replied, "If Teddy doesn't pick him up by the tail or put him in a *cage*, he will run in and out of the house all day. Let's give him some food."

They gave Rikki-tikki some meat which he liked very much. When he had finished, he decided to dry himself in the sun. Now he was feeling much better and decided to explore the house for the rest of the day. That was a real adventure. Once he nearly *drowned* himself in the bath and later burnt his nose on the big man's cigar when he climbed onto the table. When Teddy went to bed, Rikki-tikki went with him. But he found it difficult to relax with so many new noises around him. When Teddy's mother and father came into the bedroom to look at their son sleeping, they saw Rikki-tikki awake on the *pillow*.

mongoose

tailor-bird

musk-rat

cage

tame, not wild
cage, a prison for animals, especially birds
drown, to die under water
pillow, where you put your head when you are in bed

43

"I don't like that," said the mother, "he could *bite* the child."

"He won't do that," said her husband, "Teddy is perfectly safe with him. And if a snake came into the bedroom, the mongoose ..." But he stopped when he saw the nervous look in her eyes.

The next morning Rikki-tikki had breakfast with his new family. They gave him some pieces of banana and egg. He remembered the stories his mother told him and his brothers and sisters of when she lived in a white man's house. Every mongoose dreams of living in a house with people and lots of rooms. Rikki-tikki was feeling happy.

After breakfast, he went to look around the garden. It was perfect for hunting. There were lots of fruit trees, long grass and bamboo plants. Rikki-tikki was very excited and his tail got more *bushy* as he thought about it. As he *sniffed* around his new territory, he suddenly heard some birds crying from one of the trees. It was Dharzee, the tailor-bird, and his wife. Rikki-tikki could see them sitting on the *edge* of their nest, crying.

"Why are you crying?" asked Rikki-tikki.

"One of our babies fell from the nest and Nag ate him," said Dharzee.

"Oh, that is very sad," said Rikki-tikki, "but, tell me, who's Nag?"

But what Rikki-tikki heard next was not Dharzee and his wife. It was the cold *hiss* of a snake that sur-

bite, attack with teeth
bushy, like a brush or a small tree
sniff, here, to investigate with your nose
edge, the outside part
hiss, the noise a snake makes

44

prised him so much that he jumped a metre in the air.
Slowly he saw the head of a big, black cobra appear
from the long grass. This was Nag and, from head to
tail, he was two metres long. Nag lifted his head and
moved the top part of his body from side to side, like a   5
flower in the *breeze* and watched Rikki-tikki with his
cold, hard eyes.

"Who is Nag?" he hissed, "I am Nag. And **you**, mongoose, should be afraid."

In fact Rikki-tikki was afraid at first as he watched   10
the marks and colours on the cobra's *hood*. This was

breeze, a gentle wind
hood, here, the wide part of a cobra's neck

Rikki-tikki's first contact with a real, live cobra. Of course his mother gave him dead ones to eat. He knew, too, that a mongoose spends his whole life fighting snakes so he was not afraid for long. No mongoose can
5 live with snakes in his garden for long. Nag knew this too and, in the bottom of his cold heart, he was nervous.

"So why does a big snake like you eat *defenceless* little baby birds?" Rikki-tikki asked.
10 Nag waited before he replied and watched the long grass behind Rikki-tikki. He knew that one day the mongoose would kill him and his family. He needed to be very careful and try to attack when Rikki-tikki was unprepared.
15 "You mongooses eat eggs. Why can I not eat birds?" he asked, still watching the grass.

"Behind you!" sang Dharzee from his nest.

Rikki-tikki did not look around but jumped high up into the air, feeling the head of Nag's wife, Nagaina, fly

defenceless, with no defence

46

close by him. Rikki-tikki came down on her back and quickly bit her neck but not enough to kill Nagaina. An older mongoose would have killed her without waiting but Rikki-tikki was young and not sure how the snake's head was going to move. He quickly jumped clear of Nagaina's tail as she escaped into the grass.

"Stupid, stupid bird!" hissed Nag and jumped up towards Dharzee's nest but it was too far away for snakes.

Rikki-tikki's eyes were going red and hot, which shows that a mongoose is angry. But it was too late as the two snakes were already away into the grass. Rikki-tikki did not follow them. Two snakes at the same time was too difficult. He went to sit outside the house and think a little about the situation. He knew that in a fight between a mongoose and a snake the most important thing was *speed*. The speed of the mongoose's jump and the snake's attacking head. Rikki-tikki was pleased that, in his first fight against a cobra, he escaped a surprise attack from behind. Next time he was going to be ready for them. As he started to feel happier, Teddy ran out of the house. Rikki-tikki was waiting for his new friend to pick him up when he saw something move in the grass. A little voice said, "Be careful! I am Death". Karait was a small snake that liked to lie in the sun. He is very difficult to see but his bite is more dangerous than the cobra's.

Rikki-tikki's eyes quickly went red again as he danced from side to side towards the killer-snake. It is more difficult to kill a small snake as they can move very quickly so Rikki-tikki needed to be careful. But

speed, how fast you move

Rikki-tikki did not know this. His eyes were all red and waited for the snake's attack. Karait threw his head at Rikki-tikki who jumped to one side. The little snake attacked again immediately and almost bit the
5 mongoose's *shoulder*.

Teddy shouted to the house, "Look, Mum, Dad! Our mongoose is fighting with a snake." Teddy's mother *screamed* and his father ran out with a *stick*. But before he got there Rikki-tikki was on the snake's back and
10 biting as high as possible into the snake's neck. With this bite the snake was *paralysed* and Rikki-tikki thought of eating him. Then he remembered that a fat mongoose is a slow mongoose and he needed his speed for the cobras. He jumped away and watched the man
15 hit the dead snake with his stick. Then all the family looked at Rikki-tikki as the father said, "We are very lucky. This mongoose has saved little Teddy's life." Rikki-tikki was amused by all the attention they gave him.

At supper that evening the family tried to give him
20 some very nice things to eat but Rikki-tikki was thinking of Nag and Nagaina. Sometimes his eyes went red and he shouted his mongoose *war-cry*, "**Rikki-tikk-tikki-tikki-tchk!**"

After supper Teddy carried him up to bed. Rikki-tik-
25 ki waited for the boy to sleep and went for a walk around the house. In the living-room he saw the muskrat, Chuchundra. Chuchundra was a timid and nervous creature that spent his life walking around the edge of

30 *shoulder*, the top part of your arm, next to your neck
scream, to shout very loudly
stick, a piece of wood from a tree
paralysed, it could not move
war-cry, something you shout when you enter a battle

48

rooms.

"Don't kill me, please, Rikki-tikki!" he said with *tears* in his eyes.

"Snake-killers don't kill musk-rats," said the mongoose. 5

"But one dark night Nag may think that I am you and kill me."

"That will never happen. Nag lives in the garden and you never go there."

"Yes," said Chuchundra, "but my cousin Chua said ... " 10

"**What** did Chua say?"

"Oh, no! I can't tell you. Nag is everywhere. Can't you **hear**, Rikki-tikki?" Chuchundra asked as the tears ran down his face.

Rikki-tikki listened. At first there was nothing but 15 then he heard it. The hard, dry sound of a snake moving over *bricks*. He knew that it was Nag or Nagaina and that they were going into the bathroom through a hole in the bathroom wall. As he listened outside the bathroom, Rikki-tikki heard the two cobras *whispering* 20 in the moonlight.

"When there are no people in the house," said Nagaina to her husband, "**he** will go away, too, and then the garden will be for us again. You go in and first bite the man who killed Karait. After that we will look 25 for Rikki-tikki together."

"But do we need to kill the humans?" asked Nag.

"Of course. Before the people came there was no mongoose in our garden. And when our eggs in the

tear, water that comes from your eyes when you cry
brick, a block used for building
whisper, talk very quietly

melon-garden *hatch*, - and that could be tomorrow - our children will need peace and quiet."

"You're right, Nagaina. I will go and kill the big man, but we will not have to find Rikki-tikki. If I also kill the boy and his mother, the mongoose will leave the empty house."

Rikki-tikki's eyes began to go red as he heard this. As he saw the giant cobra's head looking around the bathroom with its eyes shining in the light from the moon, Rikki-tikki thought about what to do next. On the open floor the snake had an advantage, especially if Nagaina was outside waiting. "What will I do?" Rikki-tikki asked himself.

Then he heard Nag say to himself, "Yes, yes. This morning the man had a stick but when he comes here tomorrow for his bath he will not bring it. I will wait until he comes. Do you hear me, Nagaina?"

There was no answer so Rikki-tikki knew that Nagaina had gone. Nag climbed into the big water-jar the family used for filling the bath and slowly fell asleep. Rikki-tikki watched for more than an hour in complete silence. "He has a big back and it will be dif-

melon, a big, heavy fruit
hatch, the young snakes break open their eggs to get out

50

ficult for me to break with one jump," he thought, "and if I jump close to the tail he can still bite me. I will attack his head above the hood but I must not *let go*."

Nag's head was hanging outside the water-jar. Rikki jumped and bit so hard into Nag's head that his teeth 5 closed together. Nag was jumping all around the floor and crashing Rikki-tikki against the walls, the floor

---

let go, release, stop biting

and the side of the bath. He thought he was going to die but, for the *honour* of his family, continued to bite as hard as he could. Then he heard a loud BANG! and felt something hot burn his fur a little. The man was standing over him with a big gun in his hand. Rikki-tikki was not sure if he was dead or alive but kept his teeth together. Then the big man picked him up and said, "It's the little mongoose again, Alice. This time he has saved **our** lives."

Rikki-tikki climbed slowly onto Teddy's bed and quickly fell asleep.

Next morning, with his body *aching*, Rikki-tikki felt very pleased with his work from the day before. "But now I have Nagaina and her eggs to think about," he said to himself. "I must speak to Dharzee."

He found Dharzee singing from the top of his tree. It was a victory song. The animals in the garden saw the house-cleaner throw the dead Nag out with the *rubbish* earlier that morning.

"Be quiet, you stupid bird!" shouted Rikki-tikki.

"But you have killed Nag and he will never eat my babies again," sang Dharzee.

"Yes, yes. But where's Nagaina? Have you seen her?" But Dharzee continued to sing his victory song, "The great red-eyed Rikki-tikki has killed Nag. He's dead, dead, dead!"

"Oh, shut up, Dharzee and for the last time, where's Nagaina?"

"She is crying next to the rubbish for her dead husband, you great killer of the terrible Nag."

honour, good name, reputation
ache, to hurt or be painful
rubbish, waste

52

"And her eggs. Have you seen her eggs?" Rikki-tikki said with *impatience*.

"They are in the melon-garden, next to the wall, where the sun shines," explained Dharzee.

"I need your help. Fly over to the rubbish and tell Nagaina that your wing is broken. When she tries to catch you, I will go to the melon-garden."

Dharzee was a stupid, little bird and did not think it very nice to kill little eggs. After all, birds had eggs, too. His wife was more intelligent and knew that her family was not safe with baby cobras in the garden. She left Dharzee to keep the eggs warm and sing his victory song. She found Nagaina crying next to the body of her dead husband and started crying, at some distance from Nagaina.

"Oh, dear! My wing is broken. Help me, Nagaina! The boy has hit me with a stone."

"You told Rikki-tikki when I was going to kill him. This is really not a good day for you to have a broken wing," Nagaina hissed.

"The boy hit me with a stone!" cried Dharzee's wife.

"Yes. I will see the little boy later. But now, look at me, you little fool. I am going to eat you."

The bird knew that to look a snake in the eye is certain death and continued to jump away from the snake with just one wing as Nagaina moved closer and closer.

At the same time Rikki-tikki ran to the melon-garden and found the twenty-five eggs in a warm place near the wall. He could see the baby cobras through the thin walls of the eggs. One by one he broke the eggs and killed the baby cobras inside. Then he saw

---

impatience, not wanting to wait

53

Dharzee's wife again.

"Quick, Rikki-tikki, she is inside the house. Come quickly!" she cried.

He ran to the house carrying the last egg in his mouth. As he got to the door he saw the family sitting at the breakfast table with very white faces. Nagaina was very close to Teddy's leg and moving her head from side to side, waiting to attack.

"Now I will kill the son of the big man who killed my Nag. *Foolish*, foolish people!"

Teddy watched his father. "Don't move, Teddy. Sit very, very still."

Then Rikki-tikki moved closer. "Turn and fight, Nagaina!"

"I will kill you later. First I kill your friends."

"Think of your eggs, Nagaina. Are they still in the melon-garden?"

The big snake turned around and saw one of her eggs on the floor in the doorway.

"Give me my egg, **NOW**!" she screamed.

But Rikki-tikki put his paws on top of the egg, his eyes as red as blood. "What would you give for the last of your baby cobras? The last egg. The ants are eating the others."

Now she turned around and moved away from the table towards her last egg. Teddy's father jumped up and pulled the boy away from the snake.

"Ha! Ha! Now the boy is safe, Nagaina, and it was me that killed your Nag, not the man's gun. Come, come and fight with me. Soon you will be on the rubbish with your dead husband."

| *foolish*, stupid

54

"Give me the egg, Rikki-tikki. I will leave and never return if you give me my egg," cried Nagaina, moving slowly closer to her last baby. Rikki-tikki jumped up and down and from side to side waiting for Nagaina to attack him. At last it came. Once, twice, three times 5 she threw herself at him. Each time she missed as Rikki-tikki jumped away from her flying head. As his eyes grew redder, Rikki-tikki danced in a circle around the cobra. But he forgot the egg. Nagaina moved closer to it and, while Rikki-tikki continued to dance around 10 her, quickly picked the egg up in her mouth and flew out of the house like an *arrow*. Rikki-tikki ran after her.

arrow, a pointed stick, used for hunting

He knew he had to kill Nagaina and her egg. She quickly began to disappear into a rat-hole in the garden, knowing that a mongoose never fights a snake in a hole. Rikki-tikki bit the tail before it disappeared and used his legs to try and stay out of the hole. But Nagaina continued to pull. Then the earth around the hole stopped moving and Dharzee said, "Poor Rikki-tikki. That is the end of the brave red-eyed mongoose. I will sing a song for his death. Nagaina will surely kill him underground."

Then, as he was in the middle of the sad song, he saw the grass begin to move again and the head of Rikki-tikki appeared, covered in earth. "That's it. No more cobras. Now you can tell all the others." With that news all the red ants began to hurry down into the rat-hole to see.

He fell asleep in the grass. It had been a long day. When he woke up, he walked into the house where the family cried with happiness when they saw him. He ate everything they gave him - bananas, eggs, meat and more - and later went to bed on little Teddy's shoulder.

Rikki-tikki was a *proud* mongoose but never too proud. He continued to jump, bite and dance and to keep the garden as a mongoose should keep it - free from snakes. No cobra appeared inside its walls again.

proud, pleased with himself

TIGER-TIGER!

After Mowgli's fight with the Pack at Council Rock, he decided it was a good time to move away for a while. He ran down the hill until he saw the village in the fields next to the jungle but thought that it was too close to home. He continued his run, another twenty kilometres, until he came to a country he did not know. At one end of a valley he saw a village and at the other the jungle which stopped suddenly before a wide, flat area of fields. Here, he saw cows and buffaloes in the grass. Some boys who were watching the animals ran away when they saw Mowgli come closer. As he walked towards the village, the dogs began to *bark*. Then he saw that the villagers had put some bushes across the road as a defence.

He sat next to the bushes until a man came out. Mowgli stood up and opened his mouth, pointing with his finger to show the man that he was hungry. The man stopped and watched *in terror* before running away and shouting to the village *priest*. A big fat man with a

priest

bark, noise made by dogs
in terror, very afraid
priest, the religious leader of the village

red and yellow mark on his head came and stood in front of about a hundred people, all watching and pointing at Mowgli.

"These Men are worse than the Bandar-log," thought Mowgli.

"Why are you afraid?" shouted the priest to the others. "Look at the marks on his arms and legs. He is only a wolf-child."

One of the women shouted, "Poor boy! So handsome and bitten by wolves. But see his eyes - they are as wild as fire. Messua, look at him. He looks very much like your son that was taken by the tiger."

One of the women, with *bracelets* on her wrists and ankles, moved closer to Mowgli.

"Hmm. He is not my son. Look how thin he is. But his face is like my son's. It is true."

The fat priest was not a stupid man and knew very well that the woman Messua was married to the richest man in the village. He looked towards the sky, raised his arms, then put his hands slowly together before saying, "What the jungle has taken, the jungle has given back. Take the boy, sister, and do not forget to pay your thanks to Him who sees so far."

"This is like the Looking Over of the new cubs at Council Rock," thought Mowgli. "Well, if I am going to be a man, a man I will be."

The woman walked with him into her hut. Inside there were coloured cloths, big cooking pots, a Hindu

bracelet

58

statue and a mirror on the wall. She gave him some hot milk and bread and put her hand on his head. Was this really the son that the tiger took away?

Mowgli felt uncomfortable. This was the first time he had been under a roof. But he saw that it was easy to escape if he needed to. Also he found it difficult to understand Man-talk. He was good at *imitating* animals, though, and copied every word Messua said perfectly. Before it was dark he knew the names of many of the strange objects in the house.

Mowgli had a problem at bedtime. He had never slept on a bed before and he jumped out of the window when Messua closed the door. Messua's husband told her to be calm. "If he is our son and the jungle has given him back, we will see him again tomorrow."

Before Mowgli fell asleep in the grass, he felt a wet nose touching his face. "At last! I have found you, Little Brother. Already you smell like a man," Grey Brother said as Mowgli got up and put his arm around the wolf's neck.

"There is news from the jungle. Listen. Shere Khan went away with his burnt tail to hunt, but roared that he was going to find you and kill you," said Grey Brother.

"Thank you for coming with your news," said Mowgli. "I will never forget you. But I will also never forget that the Pack sent me away."

"Man, too, may send you away, Little Brother," said the wolf. "Their talk is as empty as the talk of frogs in a river. But remember this. I will wait here every day in these trees if you ever need me. "

| *imitate*, copy, do the same

59

Mowgli did not leave the village for months. He learned the language of the villagers and the games of their children. In the jungle he was small and weak but these other man-cubs found him as strong as a bull. He 5 did not understand many of the strange customs of the village. Messua's husband often had to give money to the priest or offer food to the priest's gods when Mowgli did something to offend one of the villagers. After some time they decided that Mowgli could help the 10 other boys to look after the buffaloes and cows the next day. He was very happy about that. Now that he was a working villager he was allowed to sit with the others at their club, which met under a big tree. The older men of the village sat down and told stories of gods and 15 men and ghosts. Many of the stories were about animals and the jungle which was, of course, very close. The village hunter, Buldeo, often sat with his gun next to him and told stories of his fights with the big animals.

20 Mowgli found these stories very silly and had to stop himself from laughing at the old hunter. Buldeo began to tell the others about a ghost-tiger that carried away men in the middle of the night.

"It once ate the body of Purun Dass, the evil money 25 lender," he said. "I know because he had a bad leg and this tiger also has a problem walking."

"This is very true," said the older men of the village through their grey beards.

"Rubbish!" shouted Mowgli. "He walks that way 30 because he was born like that. Everybody knows that only children could think this stupid tiger has the spirit of a money-lender."

The villagers sat in silent surprise and turned their

eyes from Mowgli to Buldeo, who finally said, "Big talk
from the little jungle-boy. Perhaps, if he is so clever, he
should take the skin of this stupid tiger to Khanhiwara.
The government there is offering a hundred *rupees* for
his life. Or perhaps he should just keep his mouth shut 5
when the *elders* speak."

"I have sat here all evening listening to Buldeo's stupid stories. He knows nothing of the jungle or the animals. How can you believe his stories of ghosts, gods
and spirits?" said Mowgli as he walked away. 10

The next morning Mowgli and the other village

rupee, the money used in India
elders, the older people of the village

boys took the cows and buffaloes out to eat grass near the river. He sat on the back of Rama, the big leader of the buffaloes with long horns and wild eyes. Mowgli made it clear that he was the master and told the oth-
5 er boys to stay with the cows while he took the buffa-loes to the wet land by the Waingunga river. The buf-falo likes to sit all day in the warm mud, only leaving his eyes and nose above the water. Mowgli climbed down off Rama's neck and went to find Grey Brother in
10 the bamboo trees.

"At last!" said the wolf. "I have been here for many days. So now you look after cows?"

"It's an order from the villagers," said Mowgli. "Is there news of Shere Khan?"

15 "He is away hunting at the moment but he plans to kill you." replied Grey Brother.

"Good. But you or one of the Brothers must sit on that rock there. Then I can see you when I leave the village. If he comes back, you must wait by the big tree
20 in the fields."

Mowgli left Grey Brother and slept under the trees near the buffaloes. Looking after cows and buffaloes is a *lazy* job. The boys spend all day sleeping, playing sol-

buffalo (Rama)

---

lazy, not very active and, here, difficult

diers or making baskets from dry grass. When evening comes, the buffaloes climb out of their mud-bath and the boys take their animals slowly back towards the lights of the village.

This was the story every day for some weeks. Every day he saw a wolf sitting on a rock in the distance and knew that Shere Khan was still away. A day came when there was no wolf and Mowgli found Grey Brother sitting under the big tree in the fields.

"Shere Khan came back last night. Tabaqui was with him." said Grey Brother.

"I am not afraid of Shere Khan but Tabaqui is very clever," said Mowgli.

"You need not be afraid of Tabaqui," said Grey Brother, licking his lips, "but before his back was broken he told me that Shere Khan was going to wait for you outside the village tonight. Now he is waiting for you in the dry *canyon* of the Waigunga."

"Has he eaten?" asked Mowgli. He knew that a hungry Shere Khan was too dangerous for him.

"Yes. He killed a pig this morning and has been drinking, too," replied Grey Brother.

"What a stupid tiger!" said Mowgli. "And he thinks he will attack me after he has slept well. We must attack him now with the buffaloes. It's a pity I cannot

canyon

63

speak their language. Is there any way we can follow his smell so that the buffaloes will attack him?"

"He swam a long way down the Waigunga so we will never find it," said the wolf.

5 Mowgli thought carefully for a moment. "We will have to block the other end of the canyon. Grey Brother, can you divide the buffaloes into two groups?"

"No, but I know someone who can," Grey Brother replied and looked away towards the trees where they 10 both saw the head of another wolf.

Akela was there to offer his help. Together he and his younger helper *howled* before running into and separating the buffaloes. In one group were the cows with their young and in the other the bulls. Cows with their 15 *calves* are more dangerous than the bulls alone, of course.

"Grey Brother, you take the cows to the other end of the canyon. Akela and I will stay here with the bulls," said Mowgli.

20 "How far into the canyon do we go?" asked Grey Brother.

"Until the sides are so high that a tiger cannot climb out," was Mowgli's reply. "Keep them there until we arrive with the others."

25 Grey Brother turned to the cows who ran towards him to attack him. He was fast enough to stay in front of them and they followed him quickly towards the other end of the canyon. Akela and Mowgli went in the other direction. The other village boys saw what 30 was happening and ran back to the village, telling the

howl, the cry of a wolf
calf, (plural calves) young cow

64

villagers that the buffaloes had run away. Mowgli took the bulls to the top of the canyon. From there he could see that the sides of the canyon were so high that a fat tiger could not climb out. They let the bulls rest for some time before Mowgli shouted down into the can- 5 yon. The echoes came back from the rocks and soon they could hear the sound of an angry and sleepy tiger.

"Who calls?" roared Shere Khan as some birds flew up out of the canyon.

"It is your friend Mowgli! Come sheep-killer, it is 10 time to return to Council Rock. Akela, quick, we must run the buffaloes down through the canyon."

The buffaloes ran down at full speed and soon they could smell a tiger. The eyes of the buffaloes and their loud *bellowing* showed their anger. The last thing Shere 15 Khan wanted to do after his big meal was to fight. He heard the buffalo bulls bellowing above and the cows below him. He ran up and down looking at the sides of the canyon. They were much too high. He turned to face the bulls now running at him through the narrow 20 pass. Behind him he could hear the cows charging at him. Mowgli, sitting on Rama's back, felt the buffalo fall over something soft. Behind him the other bulls ran over Shere Khan before crashing into the cows coming in the other direction. The wolves then ran the buffa- 25 loes out of the canyon and stopped them in some fields. Mowgli ran back to find Shere Khan lying dead on the ground.

"A dog's death. His skin will look good on the Council Rock," he said to himself. 30

Taking his knife from around his neck he quickly

bellow, the noise of buffaloes

began to cut the tiger's skin off. The wolves came back to help him with their teeth, pulling where he told them. After an hour or more, he felt a hand on his shoulder. He looked up and saw Buldeo standing there with a gun in his hand. He had come to *scold* Mowgli for not looking after the buffaloes. The wolves hid from his view.

"What are you doing, silly boy? How did the buffaloes kill the tiger? Leave that! You do not know how to skin a tiger. Ha! It is the one with the bad leg. Leave him to me! You can have one of the hundred rupees they will give me in Khanhiwara."

"Leave the tiger to me, old fool!" said Mowgli. "The skin is mine and they will not see it in Khanhiwara."

"What talk is this from a boy to the hunter of the village?" shouted Buldeo. "Your luck and the stupid buffaloes have killed this tiger. Now you have lost yourself the rupee, little idiot! Now get away and leave it to me!"

"Go away yourself, you stupid old monkey! Akela! This fool is making me angry."

In two seconds Buldeo was lying on the floor with a wolf standing over him. Buldeo was very afraid of this magic and hoped his gods would help and protect him. He lay still, waiting for the boy to change and suddenly become a jungle animal.

"Maharaj! Great King," he said finally through closed teeth.

"Yes?" said Mowgli, smiling.

"Please let me go. I did not know you were a great king. I thought you were a little village boy. Tell your

scold, to tell someone you are angry with them

servants not to kill me, please!"

"You can leave him, Akela," said Mowgli, still cutting.

Buldeo ran away as fast as he could to the village, looking back every ten metres. Once in the village, he told the priest a fantastic story of evil magic. After some hours Mowgli hid the skin and with the wolves' help started to take the buffaloes back to the village. It was dark now and as they got closer, Mowgli saw the villagers standing with lights in their hands, waiting for him. "They are happy that I have killed Shere Khan," he thought to himself but then a stone flew past his ear.

"Stay out Jungle Devil! Wolf-Child! Quick, Buldeo! Shoot him with your gun!" they shouted.

A shot was fired and a young buffalo fell to the floor.

"More black magic! He can turn bullets!" shouted one of the villagers.

"What are they doing, these idiots?" asked Mowgli.

"They are much like the Pack. I think they are try-ing to make you leave," said Akela quietly.

"Again? Last time because I was a man and now because I am a wolf. Come, Akela, we will leave."

A woman ran from the group of villagers to Mowgli.

"My son! My son!" shouted Messua. "You must leave. Buldeo says you are an evil *magician* who can change into an animal. Go away or they will kill you!"

"Come away, Messua, or you will die, too," shouted one of the villagers as a stone hit Mowgli on the mouth.

"Go back, Messua. These fools and their stupid mon-

magician, person who is skilled in the art of magic; good at entertain-ing people

68

key-stories. I am no magician. Run quickly, Messua. I have paid for your son's life. Now I will send in the buffaloes. "

Akela howled and the buffaloes ran into the village, sending the villagers in all directions. 5

He turned away and ran slowly in the dark back to Council Rock. "Now I am free again, Akela. Now we will take the skin back to Council Rock." Back in the village, Buldeo's story was getting more and more fantastic. In the end he told the other elders how Akela 10 had stood on two legs and talked like a man.

"They threw me out of the Man Pack, Mother," said Mowgli as he walked into Mother Wolf's cave. "But I have brought Shere Khan's skin as I promised."

The old she-wolf walked in front of her sons to the 15 Council Rock with tears in her eyes.

"I remember the day Shere Khan put his head inside our cave the first time, little frog. I told him then that one day the hunter would be hunted. It is well done."

"Yes, it is well done," said another deep, strong 20 voice, from the trees. "Welcome back, little brother." Bagheera walked with the wolves and watched as Mowgli put the tiger skin on Akela's rock.

"Look well, Wolves," he said, as he had said the first time Mowgli was presented to the Pack. Since Akela 25 was no longer their leader, the wolves did not eat so well and many of them had *injuries* from lost battles. They were very happy to see Shere Khan's skin on the Rock.

"You must be our leader again, Great Akela," said 30 one of them, "and you too, man-cub, so that we can be

| *injury*, wound

69

the Free People again."

"No," said Mowgli. "Man pack and wolf pack have sent me away. Now I will hunt alone in the jungle."

"And we will go with you," said the four brothers.

5   So it was that Mowgli went away and hunted alone with the four wolves. But he was not always alone. One day he even got married.

But that is another story.

THE *UNDERTAKERS*

"Respect the *Aged!*" shouted a thick, muddy and very frightening voice. "Respect the Aged, friends of the river! Respect the Aged!"

But the owner of the voice could not be seen in the muddy waters of the Ghaut. There were only a few small boats carrying stone under the railway bridge and they were some distance down-river.

The wide Indian river looked more like a line of little lakes. The water moved very slowly and now, in the dry season, the little rivers that ran into the big one were not carrying water. On the left side of the river there was a small village with one street that ended at the river. Where the street stopped the villagers often came to wash. The lands next to the village were full of rice and cotton which grows after the rainy season when the river *rises*.

As it got darker, hundreds of birds flew down to sleep in the fields. The last bird to arrive was an old and slow-moving *adjutant crane*.

"Respect the Aged!" said the voice again.

The Crane turned slowly in the direction of the voice and finally landed on a sand-bar in the middle of the river. He was a big, old bird, nearly two metres tall, but he was losing his feathers and the bag he had under his *beak* for carrying food was just *bare* skin. He moved his

undertaker, a person who takes away and buries the dead
aged, old people
rise, to go up
adjutant crane, see picture, page 74
beak, see picture, page 74
bare, here; naked

71

legs very lightly as he cleaned his grey tail-feathers. He was very proud of his legs.

A Jackal, whose hair was beginning to fall out, ran across the *shallow* water to where the Crane stood on one
5 leg. This was a very poor and dirty Jackal who got his food from the rubbish in the villages. He was always hungry and never stopped trying to show how clever he was. Nobody had much time for him.

"I hope those dogs die of something horrible," he said
10 as he pulled himself out of the mud. "See where they bit me. And just because I was looking at a shoe."

"I hear the shoe had a small *puppy* inside." said the Crane as he looked away.

"To hear is not to know," replied the Jackal. He got all
15 his clever *sayings* from the men in the villages.

"That's true," said the Crane, "so I looked after the puppy while the dogs were busy with you."

At that point, the Jackal saw the water moving a little in the river. "Life is difficult for us all at these times.
20 Even our excellent master, the Lord of the River -"

"Liars, *flatterers* and jackals all come from the same egg," said the Crane, looking at his feathers. He was not famous for his honesty either, though.

"The Lord of the River," continued the Jackal, still
25 watching the dark water. "Even he finds it difficult to get food with this new bridge. But he, with his great intelligence and strength, maybe finds it a little less difficult than me, for I am weak and stupid."

Suddenly there was a noise like a small boat arriving

shallow, not deep
puppy, a baby dog
sayings, proverbs, popular expressions or clichés
flatter, to say nice things to someone so that they like you

and the Jackal turned to look at the creature he was talking about. In front of him lay a six-metre-long, man-eating crocodile.

"What a nice surprise! I was just talking about you, Great One and Protector of the Poor. I hope you did not hear me," said the Jackal. 5

Of course the crocodile heard the Jackal and knew that he was only flattering him. But he was always happy to hear it.

"Respect the Aged and the Sick!" he said quietly as he 10 pulled himself onto the sandy bank, his red eyes burning on each side of his triangular head. Slowly, he made himself look like a large piece of wood lying on the sand.

"It is difficult to hear anything, my boy," said the crocodile, "when your ears are full of water and you are as 15 weak with hunger as I am. Since the people of the village built the bridge they don't love me any more."

"People! They are all the same," said the Jackal.

"Oh, no, you are very wrong. They are very different," replied the crocodile. "Some are very thin, others are, 20 erm, fat as young jack-, I mean, dogs. All of them are very good. Men, women and children."

"But what *ingratitude* they have shown you, Excellent One!" continued the Jackal.

"No, not ingratitude. They never think of others, 25 that's the problem. When I see how those little, fat children cannot climb down the steps to wash in the river, tears come to my eyes. But when the bridge is no longer new I am sure we will see their meaty, brown legs in the river," said the crocodile. 30

"But they do think of you," said the Crane. "Only this

ingratitude, what you show when you do not thank somebody

73

crocodile

beak

jackal

adjudant crane

74

morning I saw a woman throwing flowers into the river in your honour."

"Old fool!" said the crocodile. "She is almost blind and saw a piece of wood in the river. I watched her to see if she was going to walk a little closer to me. Still, the thought was very honourable."

"Flowers! What use are they to **me**? You can't eat flowers when you are looking through the rubbish," said the Jackal, always watching his Protector of the Poor.

"Nothing wrong with rubbish," said the crocodile. "Five times I have seen the river destroy the village and five times they have built the village again and every time they have named the village after me - *Mugger*-Ghaut. When the river rises again, there will be more rubbish for us all. All good things come to he who waits, as they say."

"I've spent my life waiting and what do I get? Kicks and bites!" the Jackal complained.

"Ho! Ho! The famous patience of the jackal! It is as great as his honesty. Ho! Ho!"

The Crane could be very cruel sometimes but his hard and pointed beak stopped the cowardly Jackal from doing anything about it. Instead, he decided to annoy the crocodile.

"They say you once made a mistake," he said, still watching the Mugger out of the corner of his left eye.

"The mistakes of my youth, perhaps," replied the crocodile, "when I was not as large nor as experienced as I am now. But you are right, I made one mistake once, at the end of a very long dry season. I was very hungry then, no different from the other animals or the villag-

Mugger, an Indian name for the meat-eating crocodile

75

ers. Anyway, when it finally rained I was so happy and, as I said, hungry that I swam up river and out into the flooded rice-fields. There was a lot of food in the fields. I was not careful enough with what I was putting in my
5 mouth, though, and some glass bracelets and a shoe made me feel quite uncomfortable for some time after."

The Jackal could only listen with considerable *envy*. "I ate very well that day," continued the crocodile, "but didn't notice the water going down as the flood ended. I
10 had to walk back through the village through the mud. Not the best place to do battle for a mugger like myself. And then a man came out with an *axe* telling the villagers that I was the Mugger of the Ghaut and that he would kill me. But the priest stopped him. "No, wait!
15 Can you not see that he is a river-god and that he takes the flood away with him," he said. So it was that they began to throw flowers to me and a *hairy goat* which I made some room for."

"Mmmm. How I love goat!" declared the Jackal.

20 "And some time later the axe-man came looking for me to cut off my tail. But luck was not with him. His boat got *stuck* on the sand and he decided to sleep there until the next day. He didn't live to see the next day,

axe   hairy goat

envy, wanting something you cannot have
stuck, it could not move

though. I followed his empty boat down river and waited for other men to go and look for it. Sure enough three men came. None of them went back to their village, that's for sure."

Now the Jackal's mouth and eyes were wide open in 5 admiration for so much killing and *savagery*. "What intelligence!" he said.

"Intelligence? Rubbish!" shouted the Mugger. "That is not intelligent but the result of experience. Intelligent is my cousin the fish-eater who has to know the difference 10 between all the different types of fish in the river, like the Mohoo, the Chapta, the Batchua or the Chilwa."

"All of them are equally good," said the Crane at last.

"So my cousin says," continued the crocodile, "but that sort of intelligence is not for me. My food lives on 15 the land and I have to understand the ways of my villagers. If a new baby is born, one day he will go down to the Ghaut to play. If a young girl marries, she will swim in the river before her wedding. All of this I learn by watching them. And when the river changes its course, 20 the Mugger is watching and waiting, too."

"And what for?" interrupted the Jackal. "The rivers always change their course in India. They can move hundreds of metres in a few months taking land from one side and leaving it on the other. Even I can see 25 that."

"Yes, you know that but you don't know what I know," said the crocodile. "When there is new land, the villagers want it for themselves. And when they fight for land, there is always death and a hungry mugger waiting close 30 by. *The Sikhs* have been very good to me, I have to say."

savagery, cruelty
The Sikhs, members of a Hindu religious sect

77

"Huh! They are too clean and careful for my liking," said the Crane. "No, I preferred Calcutta in the old days, before the white-faced English changed everything. Then there was much food in the streets for all of us and we could choose what we ate."

"I have heard," said the Jackal, his mouth watering, "that there were jackals down South that were as fat as pigs."

"Not now that the English are there. Their dogs keep the jackals out of Calcutta now," answered the Crane.

"Then they are no better than this lot," the Jackal complained. "I knew it. No creature on earth is friendly to a jackal."

The Crane took no notice at all of the Jackal. "I remember seeing their boats coming in. They were three times as big as your village."

"He's been as far as Delhi. He says people there walk on their heads," said the Jackal. The Mugger opened one eye wider and looked over at the Crane.

"It's true. You only lie when you hope to be believed and nobody **could** believe this," insisted the big bird. "They were taking out big pieces of white rock. When some pieces fell into the river, it slowly disappeared. The rest they put into a big house. A boatman threw me a piece no bigger than a dog and I of course *swallowed* it without thinking. But then I couldn't move with the cold inside me. From head to claws, my whole body felt almost frozen. I couldn't speak, I was so cold. And all the time the boatmen were laughing so much that they fell on the floor."

The Jackal and the Mugger had never seen ice and

swallow, to let food go down your neck without chewing first

78

found the story impossible to understand. The crocodile closed his eye again.

"With boats that size, anything is possible," he said.

At that point they heard a whistle and all turned their heads up to the railway bridge. The 21.30 train to Delhi pulled itself slowly and noisily across the bridge before disappearing into a tunnel on the other side.

"Incredible, isn't it?" said the Crane.

"I saw them building it, stone by stone. In fact I was waiting for them when they fell off. I can find nothing strange about it," declared the Mugger.

"But the thing that goes across it, that **is** strange," insisted the Crane.

"It is, of course, a new kind of bull. One day it will fall off and Mugger will be there waiting for it," said the crocodile.

The Jackal looked at the Crane and the Crane looked at the Jackal. They did not know what the thing was but they both knew it certainly was not a bull. Of course, the Mugger could only see it from down here in the river while they had seen it from higher ground.

"You're probably right," said the Jackal, "it's a new kind of bull. Yes, that's what it is, a bull."

"But it could be -" started the Mugger slowly.

"Yes, you're right, it could be," said the Jackal without thinking.

"Could be what? I didn't finish what I was saying," asked the crocodile, suspecting that the others knew more than he did. "You said before it was a bull."

"It is what the Protector of the Poor wants it to be," said the Jackal nervously.

"In any case it is work of the white-face and I have no time for them," declared the Crane.

79

"You do not know the white-faces like I know them," said the Mugger. "I remember when they were here building the bridge. One of them always came out in his boat with his gun, shooting at pieces of wood in the river and making lots of noise. That is how the English do their hunting. Fools!"

"And who hunts the English?" asked the Jackal.

"Nobody, now," replied the Mugger, "but there was a time -"

"I can remember that hunting," said the Crane, banging his long beak, "although I was a lot younger then."

"My cousin the fish-eater told me stories that convinced me to take to my feet and walk over land," said the crocodile.

"What stories?" asked the Jackal.

"I walked by night," continued the Mugger, "up the little rivers when I could but it was the dry season. I walked across roads, over hills, through long grass and finally across the land where no water runs until I finally found the rivers that flow towards the Ganges. I was more than a month from my river and my people!"

"And what did you find to eat?" asked the Jackal, who could only think of his stomach.

"It's funny that you ask me that," said the Mugger very slowly as he watched the Jackal. The Crane could see how nervous the Jackal was now and could not stop himself from laughing out loud. Finally he asked the Mugger to continue his story, which he was very happy to do.

"What lovely water there was in those rivers!" said the crocodile. "Not like the floods we get here with their dead chickens and drowned strangers. No, these waters were full of the white-faced English, just as my cousin told me. I ate so well those days. That it why I am so big

80

today, after the eating by the waters of *Allahabad*."

"Yes, those were good times," said the Crane, dancing from one leg to the other. The Jackal could not remember the year of the *Indian Mutiny*.

"Yes, there were so many then, we could pick and choose. All of us muggers were fat in those days, none as fat as me, of course," continued the crocodile. "But then they stopped coming for some time until one day we saw more white faces. This time they were alive and sailing up the river in boats. There was lots of shooting but never at us muggers. I remember one day there was a small child holding his hand down in the water. As I lifted my head, - to get a better view of him, you understand - a woman shot at me five times with a small gun. Five times! As quickly as I move this tail."

The Jackal had just enough time to jump back before the tail could hit him into the river.

"One of the bullets hit me in the neck. Why do you not have a look and see if it is still there?" the crocodile asked the Jackal.

"Oh, no, I believe you," replied the Jackal. "It is an honour for an eater of old bones like me that the great Protector of the Poor has told me that he was once shot by a woman. That will be a story for my children."

"I do not want any children of yours to hear that the Mugger of Mugger-Ghaut was hurt by a woman. You should be more careful with your words, child!" shouted the crocodile.

"Of course, I have already forgotten everything," said the Jackal. "No boat, no woman, nothing."

Allahabad, a village in India
Indian Mutiny, an Indian uprising against the English

The Mugger was annoyed that, for the second time
tonight, the Jackal had not become his latest victim.
The Jackal knew this but also that "Eat and be eaten"
was the law of the river.

5   "The river was empty for a while," said the Mugger,
"but then it began to fill again, this time with Sikhs and
Hindus, not the white-faces. All the time we could hear
the guns on both sides of the Ganges and more and more
bodies floating in the river. In the end, even I was tired
10 of so much shooting and so many boats in the river. I

came back to my village and found people the same as before, still working in the rice-fields. There were bodies here, too, but not of the English. My people said it was better to keep working and wait for the killing to stop."

"What a fantastic story!" said the Jackal. "It makes me feel fat just listening."

"Still, not everything is sunshine and roses, as they say in the village," said the Mugger.

"What is it that makes the Mugger unhappy?" asked the Crane.

"I am always sad when I think of how I missed that little white baby," said the crocodile.

"It would be horrible to think that he was telling everybody how he escaped death in the jaws of the Mugger of Mugger-Ghaut. Now I will rest and think," he continued, closing his eyes. "Keep silent, children. And respect the aged!"

The Jackal and the Crane walked away, leaving the Mugger to sleep on the sand-bar.

"All those stories of his killings," said the Jackal, looking up at the big bird, "and not once has he told me where I could find some small piece of good meat for myself."

"Be quiet!" said the Crane lifting his wing nervously. "Look over there! Two men and a gun. Not for me, though, all of India knows I am protected." The Indian Crane can go where it wants, as this one knew.

"And they would only hit me with old shoes, not bullets," said the Jackal. "No, they are white-faces. I can hear their heavy boots. They are looking for the Mugger, not us."

"Well, you should go and tell your Protector of the Poor then," said the Crane.

"Let him look after himself. He says he is not afraid of the white-faces," said the Jackal. "He can't hear so well when he is out of water. Perhaps we will eat tonight."

From the bridge a voice said quietly, "It's a difficult shot
5 from here. Try and hit him behind the neck. The villagers will be angry. This one is the river-god of these parts."

"I don't care," said the other. "He had about fifteen of my workers when we were building the bridge."

Then there was an enormous explosion as two shots of
10 the elephant-gun were fired into the sleeping crocodile. One hit him in the neck, the other above the tail. the crocodile was broken into three pieces. The two English-men ran down to the river and then through the water to the sandbank where they admired the size of the Mug-
15 ger. One of them picked up the head.

"The last time I had my hand near a Mugger's mouth," he said, "was when I was five years old, during the mutiny. My mother told me how she shot it in the head with Dad's old pistol."

20 "Well," said the other, "You've certainly got yourself a big one here. This was worth waiting all night for, wasn't it?"

Strangely, that was exactly what the Jackal and the Crane said three minutes after the men left.

LETTING IN THE JUNGLE

You will remember that Mowgli left Shere Khan's skin on the Council Rock and told the Pack that he was going to hunt alone in future. But he did not leave immediately. First of all he went back to Mother Wolf's cave to sleep. When he woke up, he told his story of life with Man to his Wolf Family. Some of it they found very difficult to understand. Akela and Grey Brother helped him to tell the story of the buffaloes and Shere Khan. Bagheera and old Baloo listened to the adventures with big smiles on their faces.

"None of this was possible without Akela and Grey Brother's help," said Mowgli. "But Mother, it was *incredible* how the Man-Pack threw stones at me. That was something to see!"

"Apart from the woman who gave you milk," said Raksha, "I have no time for any of them. I would do something terrible to them if ... "

"Relax, Raksha," said her husband. "Leave Man in peace!"

"Leave Man in peace," said the others together.

"I don't want to see Man again!" shouted Mowgli.

"But perhaps Man wants to see you," Akela said with a worried look on his face. "I went back to cover up our *tracks* after we returned with Shere Khan's skin and saw Mang, the Bat. He told me that the village was very angry and that men were carrying guns. And Man does not carry guns for *pleasure*, Little Brother. Perhaps even

incredible, not to be believed
tracks, marks left by feet in sand, for example
pleasure, fun, enjoyment

85

now there are men with guns looking for you."

"But why? They have sent me away from the Man-Pack," said Mowgli. "Is that not enough?"

"You know more than us about the ways of Man," said Akela.

Mowgli quickly took out his knife. "Never speak of Man and me at the same time again!" he said, holding the knife in front of Akela's face.

Before Akela could answer, Bagheera jumped to his feet with his nose in the air. Akela and the rest of the wolves ran up onto the rocks, their noses up to smell the wind. Mowgli, of course could never smell as well as the jungle animals, especially after his time in the village.

"Man!" said Akela to the others.

The four brothers started to run down the hill where they could see Buldeo and his gun.

"Where are you four going?" asked Mowgli.

"To kill him where he stands," said Grey Brother.

"But wait! You cannot kill Man!" shouted Mowgli.

"Ha! A minute ago you said you were a wolf!" said Akela.

"Do I have to explain everything I say?" asked Mowgli.

"That is Man speaking," said Bagheera. "We all know that Man is the most clever of us all. But sometimes, if you listen to some of the things he says, he seems to be the most stupid."

"Hunt alone, Little Brother," said Grey Brother angrily. "I am staying here."

"Are you all saying that Mowgli doesn't know what he's doing, then?" said Mowgli and began to *stare* at the

stare, to watch very closely

86

wolves, one by one. They *trembled* and dropped their eyes. "Who is the leader of us five?"

Grey Brother licked Mowgli's foot. "You are our leader, Little Brother."

"So you will do what I say," said Mowgli as he walked 5 down the hill, the wolves behind him. Very quietly they moved closer and closer to Buldeo who was looking around to find the track that Akela had covered the day before. Buldeo did not see or hear a thing and did not know that the wolves were less than a stone's throw 10 from him.

"This is fun," said Grey Brother. "Look at him. He looks like a lost pig. What is he saying?"

"He doesn't understand the tracks and says he's tired," answered Mowgli. 15

"And now what's he doing?" asked another Brother.

"Smoking a pipe," said Mowgli. "Man is always playing with his mouth."

A group of travellers walked through the trees and of course stopped to speak to Buldeo, the famous hunter. 20 As they sat and smoked their pipes, Buldeo told them of his latest adventure. He spoke of how he killed the great Shere Khan, of a devil-child who changed into a wolf and fought with Buldeo all day before changing into a small boy again. He told them that his village sent him 25 out to find and kill this devil-child and that the villagers had tied the devil-child's mother and father to the chairs in their house. When Buldeo returned, after killing the Jungle Boy, the villagers were going to torture them and burn them alive. Then they were going to 30 take their land and buffaloes. Killing evil people was not

| *tremble*, shake with fear or cold

a bad job, Buldeo told them.

"Have you seen this Wolf-child near here?" asked Buldeo. The travellers were happy to say that they had not seen him and decided that they were going to hurry to
5 Buldeo's village before the sun went down.

"I'll go with you. I must not let you walk through the jungle without good protection," said Buldeo, happy to leave. "You will be safe with me. The gods are protecting me."

10 Mowgli turned and told the others what Buldeo was saying. "I must go back to the village," he told them. "You follow Buldeo and his new friends and sing to them so that they know they are not alone," he said with a smile. "Meet me in the usual place when night comes,
15 Grey Brother."

The wolves began to howl together, helped by Bagheera. Mowgli laughed as he saw Buldeo and the other men looking around with terror on their faces. Then he ran, as fast as his legs would carry him, towards
20 the village.

When he got there, he saw all the villagers sitting around a fire, talking. He quietly walked to Messua's hut and climbed through the window. Four men sat outside the door which was closed. Inside, Messua and her hus-
25 band had *bandages* over their mouths and were tied to the chairs. Messua was suffering. The villagers had *stoned* her that morning. As Mowgli cut the bandages and ropes away, it was hard for her not to cry.

"I knew you would come, my son," she said through
30 her tears. Mowgli began to tremble a little as she held him.

bandage, piece of cotton cloth used for treating injuries.
stone, here, to throw stones at somebody as a punishment

"Why are they doing this?" asked Mowgli.

"Because I am rich and because they say that we are the mother and father of a devil!" said the husband.

"Devil? What is this devil?" asked Mowgli.

"I told you," said Messua looking at her husband. "I said he was no devil. This is my son Nathoo. The son the tiger stole from me."

Mowgli listened to the noises outside. Buldeo was back and telling his stories again.

"Talk, talk, talk," thought Mowgli to himself.

"Messua," he said. "You must leave. Think about where you will go. I am going to listen to that old fool."

He climbed quietly out through the window and moved over to where Buldeo and the others sat under their tree. Buldeo's clothes were *torn* and he had cut his arms and legs after climbing up trees to hide from the singing wolves. He was telling his usual stories of magic and singing devils, stopping now and then to drink water or to smoke.

"What clever creatures!" thought Mowgli. "They sit here listening to silly talk like the Bandar-log and leave Messua unguarded."

When Mowgli got to the hut he saw Mother Wolf waiting outside.

"Mother," said Mowgli, "what are you doing here?"

"I followed my children's singing. I wanted to see the woman that gave you milk," she said sadly.

"They want to kill her," said the boy. "You must pro-tect her as she escapes through the Jungle."

As she walked away into the grass she turned and said,

torn, from "to tear", to break material like paper, etc.

89

"Bagheera was right. Man goes to Man in the end."

Mowgli jumped into the hut again. "The villagers say they are coming with the Red - with fire and they are going to burn you when Buldeo finishes his story. You must leave now."

"We will go to Khanhiwara. We will be safe there under the English Law," said Messua as her husband looked in a hole under one of the walls. "He is getting his money to buy a horse when we are away from the village. If we leave now, the village will find us very quickly."

"Don't worry," said Mowgli, "the villagers will not follow you and you will be safe in the Jungle. Now you must leave. Ah! One more thing - you may hear a little singing as you walk. But no animal will touch you between here and Khanhiwara. The Jungle will watch you."

Messua put her arms around Mowgli's neck and cried before her husband took her away into the night. Mowgli watched them leave with a strange feeling in his stomach. At that point Bagheera arrived.

"What fun we have had today with all our singing," he said with eyes like fire. "So when does the killing begin? Watching these naked bodies running up and down trees has made me very hungry and the great Bagheera feels so strong he could break your head with one small move of his paw."

"Go on, then. Try it!" said Mowgli and looked seriously into the bright green eyes of the black panther until the red light behind them went away. Very soon Bagheera looked down at the floor.

"The smells of the night have made you excited," said Mowgli. "Listen! They are still talking under their tree. But when they come back they will find nobody here.

Ha! Ha!"

"Yes. They will find **me** here," said Bagheera. "They will not stay long if they see me sitting here."

"That's a good idea but be careful, my friend," said Mowgli. He did not want the villagers to see him and 5 went away to sleep.

Some time after, the villagers finished their talking and angry shouting was heard as they moved closer to Messua's hut. They were carrying knives and pieces of wood and walked behind Buldeo and the fat priest. 10 Bagheera was right. When they finally opened the door and looked inside, seeing the Black Panther lying on the bed with his mouth wide open, they did not stay long. Before Bagheera could lift himself off the bed, the villagers were inside their huts, pushing tables and boxes 15 against their doors. When he looked outside, the streets were empty.

Late the next day Mowgli woke and asked Bagheera

if there was any news.

"Chil the Kite tells me that the man and woman arrived safely in Khanhiwara. Another man gave them a horse in the next village so they went very quickly. They are well so now we can go back to the Jungle and find Baloo."

"First I want to speak to Hathi," said Mowgli seriously.

"Hathi the Elephant, the Master of the Jungle? But he will not move for anyone," said Bagheera.

"He will come," said Mowgli. "Tell him that Mowgli the frog wants to talk about the Battle of Bhurtpore with him."

"I will try," said the panther, "but it is not easy to tell Hathi what to do."

Some hours later, Bagheera returned and told Mowgli that the elephants were coming.

"Look! Here he comes now with his sons."

The four elephants moved quietly towards Mowgli, eating grass as they walked. Bagheera could see that Hathi, Master of the Jungle, was a little afraid of Mowgli."

"I will tell you a story I heard from Buldeo the hunter," said Mowgli, looking at Bagheera, "about how a strong and clever elephant fell into a trap and cut himself on one side."

Bagheera looked at Hathi and saw the white mark going from the top to the bottom of one of his legs.

"Men came to take him from the trap but he was so strong and so angry he broke away and escaped with his bad leg. But one day he returned with his three sons to the fields of Bhurtpore. What happened to those fields, Hathi?" asked Mowgli.

92

"We destroyed all the plants and then we destroyed the houses and any good ground we could find. You had to walk for three days to find some fields that we had not completely ruined," answered Hathi.

"And what happened to the men who lived there and ate those plants?" asked Mowgli.

"They went away. We took the roofs from their houses and let in the Jungle. Five villages there were and we let in the Jungle on all five. Even today not one man lives in those villages or eats food from the fields of Bhurtpore. But how do you know about this, Man-cub?" asked Hathi.

"A hunter from this village told me. This is the Man-pack that sent me away and wanted to kill their own brothers with the Red Flower. They are stupid and tell horrible lies about the Jungle. I hate them!"

"We shall kill them, then," said one of Hathi's sons.

"No! I do not want their bones," said Mowgli.

"And I do not want to smell their blood on my skin again," said Hathi.

"We must let in the Jungle on them, Hathi!" shouted Mowgli. "They wanted to kill the woman that gave me milk and food. I can still smell the blood of that woman who they attacked with stones. Let them find another village. Let in the Jungle, Hathi!"

So it was that Hathi decided to let the Jungle take back the village and the fields around it. He and his sons walked North, South, East and West and told the other creatures their plan. First the hungry pigs, then the foxes, deer and buffaloes began to walk through the Jungle to the village. After them came the meat-eaters who followed the others as far as the village. They formed a circle around the grass-eaters and in the centre of this cir-

cle - ten kilometres across - was the village.

It was in the middle of the night when Hathi and his sons broke down the gates of the village. Behind them the deer and buffaloes ran into the fields, eating the villagers' food as they moved. The pigs ate everything that the others left. Now and then the wolves howled so that the deer ran across the fields, destroying the *crops*.

When the villagers saw their fields the next morning, there was nothing to be done, all their crops were lost. Their buffaloes walked into the Jungle to look for food and never came back. They found their four horses lying dead, killed by a Black Panther.

That same night, the elephants walked back into the village and took the roof off the hut where the villagers kept their food. Now the village had no more food until after the Rains the following year. Some left the next day, others hoped that the priest's gods could help them. They stayed on, not wanting to leave their homes, and tried to live on fruit and nuts from the trees. But when they were only fifty metres from their village, they could see wild eyes watching them from the trees or hear wolves and other animals all around them. At night, Hathi broke down the walls of the channels that carried water from the river or the empty houses of the villagers who had left. In the end there was nothing to stay for. The gods of the Jungle were angry with them.

When the last group of villagers left, they got to the top of a hill and looked back for the last time. They could see Hathi and his sons taking roofs off houses and pushing walls over like paper. What they could not see was a boy behind the elephants, telling them what to do.

"First the outside walls, Hathi. We can finish the houses later. First the outside walls."

Some months later, after the Rains, you could see no grass or crops growing. Where before there were fields, now there was Jungle and it was impossible to see that once, not long ago, people lived there.

| *crops*, food which is grown to eat e.g. rice, vegetables

95

THE SPRING RUNNING

Mowgli was nearly seventeen years old now but the good food and exercise made him look stronger and bigger than most boys of his age. The Jungle People feared him for both his intelligence and his strength, and moved away when they heard him coming near. But the look in his eyes was still as gentle as ever, even when he was fighting. Bagheera could not understand this and asked him about it.

The boy laughed. "When I am hungry and miss the kill I am angry. When I do not eat for two days I am angry. Can you not see it in my eyes then?"

"The mouth is hungry," said Bagheera, "but the eyes say nothing. Like a stone in the rain or in the sun, always the same." Mowgli looked seriously at the Panther who, as always, looked away.

The morning sun began to rise over the hill where they sat, sending red and gold *stripes* across the wet grass and trees. The cold weather was coming to an end. Bagheera turned his nose up to the gentle *breeze* and smiled, closing his eyes a little.

"The year is turning," he said, "and the Time of New Talk is here. Even the trees are happy."

"What are you talking about, Bagheera?" asked Mowgli. "Look, the Eye-of-the-Spring (a small, red flower) is still closed and ... and why is the Black Panther lying on his back with that foolish smile on his face?"

Bagheera's thoughts were somewhere else.

"Are you listening to me?" continued Mowgli. "I said

stripes, lines, here from the rays of the sun
breeze, a soft wind

96

do you think that it is right to be making that noise and rolling in the grass? We are the Masters of the Jungle, remember."

"Of course I hear you, man-cub. There is none so strong or so wise as the great Mowgli," said Bagheera, shaking some of the winter fur off his back. Mowgli looked over to Bagheera to see if the Black Panther was making fun of him and then moved away and sat on a rock. Down in the valley he could hear a bird practising his Spring-song.

"The Time of New Talk is near," said Bagheera again.

"I heard you the first time," said Mowgli. "Why can you not sit still for five minutes? The sun is warm but you are shaking."

"Can you hear Ferao, the *woodpecker*. **He** knows," said Bagheera with a little smile. "I must begin to practise my song, too."

"Of course, your song. I remember now the last Time of New Talk. You and the others ran away and left me." Mowgli spoke with a little sadness in his voice. "When I called for Hathi the Elephant, he came two days later. I saw how he ran through the jungle, *trumpeting* in the moonlight like a mad thing. It was two days before he came to me and I am the Master of the Jungle!"

woodpecker

trumpeting, the noise an elephant makes

"But it was the Time of the New Talk," insisted Bagheera. "Listen to Ferao! He's practising hard, today."

In an Indian Jungle it is difficult to notice *the different seasons*. There seem to be only two - wet and dry. But if you look a little closer, they are all there. Spring is the best of them. It clears away all the half-dead leaves from winter and makes the grass feel young and fresh again. There seems to be one special day when everything smells old and tired. But this is followed by another, different day. Nothing **looks** different but there are new noises, new smells. Hair begins to fall from the Jungle People as they lose their winter fur. A little rain falls and you can almost hear the trees growing up towards the sunlight. The whole jungle moves and *hums*. This is what makes that special noise of Springtime. It is the noise of a happy world.

Until now, Mowgli had always enjoyed the changing seasons. He was always the first to see the Eye-of-the-Spring in the long grass. He helped the frogs and owls with their night calls. Like the other Jungle People he ran in the moonlight enjoying the warm air, sometimes thirty or forty kilometres, covered in flowers and singing all the way. Everywhere the other animals were singing or laughing and making the noises they only made at this time of the year. This was the Time of the New Talk.

But this year was different. Mowgli had a strange, heavy feeling in his stomach. When the day came and the animals passed on their songs from one to the other, Mowgli could not find his voice. A feeling of sadness came over him and he began to feel weak. All around

the different seasons: Spring, Summer, Autumn, Winter
hum, noise made by insects, for example

98

him the jungle sang but Mowgli stayed silent.

"I do not understand," said Mowgli to himself. "I have eaten good food but my stomach feels heavy. Sometimes I am hot, sometimes cold. I have said unkind things to Bagheera and my friends. Tonight I will make a spring running to the North. I need some hard exercise. And so do my brothers." 5

He called to the Four but not one answered. A tree-cat laughed at him which made him angry. He walked down the hill but none of his people saw him. They were all too busy. 10

"When the Red Flower dances, you all come running to Mowgli for help. And now you see some Eye-of-the-Spring, you forget who is the Master of the Jungle," thought Mowgli. 15

He ate alone that evening because the others were all singing or fighting somewhere. It was a clear, white night with a full moon - the moon of New Talk - shining on the rocks and pools. The new grass was soft under his feet and Mowgli ran very quickly down the hill that falls towards the *marshes* of the North. When he was tired of running he climbed through the trees, swinging and jumping past the tree flowers and their strong smells. Below he could see two *boars* fighting with eyes as red as fire and hear crocodiles roaring at each other. 20 25

Now he was happy and shouted or sang to himself as he moved from trees to grass, from grass to trees again. Soon the smell of the marsh flowers told him he was a long way from his hunting grounds. All around him he could hear the birds of the wetlands singing. They slept 30

marshes, very wet land, next to a river or lake
boars, wild pigs

very little in the Spring. At first, Mowgli felt free from the sadness of his jungle. But as he sat and rested, watching the moon slowly disappear, he began to feel even sadder than before.

5   "I have eaten *poison* and am going to die," thought Mowgli to himself. "And what do they care with all their singing? They will find me dead here in the water."

   As a tear rolled over his face, Mowgli began to feel a little better. After a while he jumped to his feet and
10 shouted.

Some buffalo climbed to their feet.

   "Man!" said one of them.

| *poison*, a dangerous substance which can kill you

"That is no man," said Mysa, the wild buffalo. "It is the naked wolf of the Seeonee Pack. On nights like this he runs around making lots of noise. Is there danger, Mowgli?"

"Is there danger, Mowgli?" repeated the boy. "Is that all you can worry about - danger? And what do you care about Mowgli, the hairless wolf who once sat on your back and ran you through the marsh?"

"Wolf?" shouted Mysa and laughed. "You are no more a wolf than those that shout in the dust over there."

"Where are you talking about?" asked Mowgli. "I know of no Man-Pack here near the marshes."

"Go North, then, and leave us in peace with your shouting. There you will find others who will listen to you."

"I will go and see this place. Think yourself lucky, Mysa. It is not every day that the Master of the Jungle visits you."

In the distance Mowgli saw a light that he first thought was a star. As he ran closer across the flat land next to the marsh, he saw that the light came from a fire.

"The Red Flower!" he thought to himself. He forgot that he was no longer in his jungle and walked *carelessly* across the open ground towards the village. When three or four dogs began to bark, Mowgli gave them one of his Wolf-cries that silenced them. He went closer to the hut where the light came from and saw a woman looking out of the door. A small child cried behind her.

"Sleep, child. It is only a jackal," she said. "Soon it will be morning."

Mowgli remembered that voice and was surprised at

---

carelessly, not caring

how easy it was to use man's talk again, "Messua! Can you hear me, Messua?"

"Who is it?" said Messua, a little nervously.

"Can't you remember?" Mowgli's mouth was dry.

5 "If it is you, what name did I give you?" said the woman, closing the door behind her.

"Nathoo! Ohé Nathoo!" said Mowgli, remembering the name they gave him when he first came to the Man-Pack.

10 "My son! You must come in," said Messua, opening the door again.

Mowgli walked into the light of the door and stood in front of her. This was the woman whose life he once saved many years before. Now her hair was grey and her 15 eyes and voice had changed.

"But you are not my son! How tall you are!" she said, looking him up and down. "You are a god of the jungle"

With his long, black hair, his dark, shining skin and his head covered in flowers, it was easy to see why she 20 said such a thing. Mowgli looked around at the kitchen, the water-jars and cooking pots, and memories came back to him.

"What would you like to eat or drink?" she asked him. "This is your home. We owe our lives to you. But are you 25 really Nathoo?"

"I am Nathoo," replied Mowgli, "but I did not know you lived here. I saw the light and came closer."

"When we left Kanhiwara," said Messua quietly, "the English helped us. We went to the village with the Eng-30 lishmen but we could not find it. It had disappeared."

"Yes. I heard something about that," said Mowgli.

"My man found work here in the fields. Enough for the two of us. We did not need much."

102

"Where is this man?" asked Mowgli, looking around.

"He died. A year ago now."

"And this one?" asked Mowgli, looking at the little boy, who was not as afraid as when Mowgli first arrived and began to play with Mowgli's knife.

"He was born two winters ago. If you are Nathoo, he is your little brother."

Mowgli took the boy away from his knife and sat him down gently. "Oh, Mother! My heart feels heavy," he said and sat on the floor.

"Take those flowers off your head. I will make you some warm milk," said Messua, taking a cooking-pot.

Mowgli held his head in his hands. He was feeling a little sick and confused. So many things had happened today. Messua gave him the milk and rested her hand on his shoulder.

"My son," she said with a warm look in her eyes. "Has anyone ever said you are the most handsome man they ever saw?"

"What?" asked Mowgli. Of course, nobody had ever said anything like that.

"It is good that I am the first. A mother should say these things. But it is true. You are a very fine man."

Mowgli turned to look at her and, without understanding why, began to laugh softly. Messua and her little boy laughed, too. The warm milk began to make Mowgli tired and he soon fell asleep. Messua covered him and left him to sleep the rest of the day. When he woke, he jumped to his feet with a knife in his hands.

Messua laughed and gave him his evening meal. It was very little for Mowgli and he looked forward to some hunting later. But now he had the little boy in his arms and Messua sat behind him, combing his blue-black hair.

Then her mouth fell open as she saw a paw under the closed door. Mowgli knew it was Grey Brother.

"Wait outside," he said. "You didn't come when I called you. Now you can wait." The paw disappeared.

5 Messua did not understand this jungle-talk and was still afraid. "Please do not bring your servants here. We live in peace here."

"There was peace on the road to Khanhiwara and even in Springtime the jungle people do not forget. I 10 must leave now," said Mowgli and opened the door.

Messua threw her arms around Mowgli's neck and began to cry.

"Come back to us, my son. I love you and look, even your brother cries to see you go."

15 "Don't worry. I will be back," said Mowgli. Looking at Grey Brother he shouted, "And you! Why did it take you so long when I called?"

"So long?" said the wolf. "It was only yesterday and it is the Time of the New Talk, remember. But what are 20 you doing here, eating and sleeping with the Man-Pack?"

As they were running out of the village, a girl in a white dress began to walk across the path in front of them. They hid in the long grass as the girl screamed. 25 Then she turned and walked away, Mowgli watching her all the way.

"Akela was right, Kaa was right and Raksha, our mother, was right," said Grey Brother.

"What are you saying?" asked Mowgli.

30 "They said Man goes to Man in the end."

"And what do you say, Grey Brother?"

"They throw you out of their village, they throw stones at you and even you say they are evil and stupid.

104

It was you who ordered the Letting in of the Jungle. It was you who spoke and sang against them."

"But what do **you** say?" repeated Mowgli.

Grey Brother ran on in silence for a while but finally spoke.

"I will follow you wherever you go. And what I say is true for my brothers. But what will you say to the Jungle?"

Mowgli slowed a little and Grey Brother ran on towards the Jungle. The wolf shouted to the Jungle People as he passed them, "The Master of the Jungle is going back to Man! Come to the Council Rock!" The Jungle People were happy and busy with the Time of the New Talk so that when Mowgli finally arrived, tired and sad, only a few of his friends were at the Rock. The Four Brothers, Baloo, who was now nearly blind, and Kaa watched him slowly come closer.

"So now you are leaving us, Man-cub," said Kaa.
5 "When we first met I said it. Man goes to Man in the end. The Jungle does not force him to leave."

"Sometimes I want to die. I lie down but cannot sleep. I feel hot inside and the cold stream does not help. The Red Flower is inside me but I have no heart for fighting,"
10 said Mowgli with his head in his hands.

"So much talk," said old Baloo. "I always said Mowgli would send Mowgli back to the Man-Pack. But who listens to an old bear? Bagheera - where is Bagheera? He knows the Law. Remember one thing, Little Frog. When
15 you are with your people and need feet, teeth, eyes or food, you are still Master of this Jungle."

"I don't know how to leave you, friends," said Mowgli.

"When we leave our skins," said Kaa, "we cannot climb into them again. That is the Law."

20 "I was here when Bagheera gave a young bull for you at the first Looking Over. But only he and I *remain* from that time. Your Wolf-Mother and Father are dead. We know what happened to Shere Khan, Akela died fighting the Red Dogs. Now there are only old bones," said
25 Baloo sadly. "The Master wants to take a new course. Who can question his reasons?"

At that point Bagheera crashed through the trees carrying a young bull.

"This is the bull that frees you, Little Brother. It took
30 longer than in the old days to hunt but now you are free. What Baloo says is true for me, too."

---

remain, stay, continue

At this point Bagheera licked Mowgli's foot. "Remember that Bagheera loved you," he said before running away into the trees. "Good Hunting, Master of the Jungle!"

"There is no more to say," said Baloo. "Go now, Little 5 Frog."

"It is hard to leave the old skin," said Kaa as Mowgli began to cry on Baloo's shoulder.

QUESTIONS AND ACTIVITIES

1. Mowgli's Brothers

Arrange the following sentences so that they are in the same order as the story:
a) Bagheera offered a bull as the price to pay for Mowgli
b) The little boy hid in a cave
c) Shere Khan tried to force Mother Wolf to give him the boy
d) The little boy escaped
e) Shere Khan attacked a village and stole a boy from his mother
f) When the little boy could stand up and walk, he went to the Looking Over
g) Tabaqui told Shere Khan where to find the boy

1. .e.
2. ...
3. ...
4. ...
5. ...
6. ...
7. ...

2. Kaa's Hunting

Understanding the text. Answer the following questions:
1) What was the Strangers' Hunting Call?
2) How many languages did Mowgli learn?

3) Baloo was Mowgli's teacher but there was one subject he did not tell the boy about. What was it?
4) What did Bagheera and Baloo think about discipline?
5) Why did Mowgli like the monkeys at first? How did his feelings change?
6) In the end, what did Mowgli think about discipline?

Word-building. Which of the following words could we use to describe Baloo, Bagheera, Kaa, the monkeys or Mowgli?

playful	vain	brave	selfish
strict	irresponsible	determined	loyal
cruel	proud	annoying	wise

Can you think of any more words to describe these characters?

3. Mowgli's Brothers (II)

Understanding the text.
1. How do we know that the wolves were afraid of Mowgli?
2. What was Bagheera's secret?
3. In this story Mowgli took a decision that changed his life. What was it?

Word-builder. We often use animals to describe human characteristics. For example, we often say "I'm as hungry as a wolf". Connect the following characteristics to the correct animal.

as strong as	a kitten
as weak as	a fox
as blind as	a bee
as brave as	a bird
as busy as	an ox
as wise as	a bat
as cunning as	a lion
as free as	an owl

4. Rikki-tikki-tavi

Understanding the text.
1. How did Rikki-tikki-tavi get to the bungalow?
2. Who started the fight between Nag and Rikki-tikki-tavi?
3. How did the other animals help?
4. Some people might say that there was no difference between Nagaina, Dharzee's wife and the woman in the house. They were all mothers looking after their babies. What do you think?

Word-building. Rikki-tikki-tavi was brave. Dharzee, on the other hand, was a bit cowardly. Find similar opposites from the list below:

strong	open-minded	thoughtful	mean
generous	nervous	big-headed	weak
modest	narrow-minded	selfish	relaxed

Which of them are good?

5. Tiger-Tiger!

Understanding the text.
1. Why did Mowgli think the villagers were like the Bandar-log?
2. How did Grey Brother show his loyalty to Mowgli?
3. What happened to Tabaqui?
4. In what ways was Mowgli helped in his fight against Shere Khan?

6. The Undertakers

Understanding the text.
1. What did the Jackal, the Crane and the Mugger have in common?
2. What did the Mugger eat when he crossed the desert?
3. From the Mugger's story, what do you think happened in Allahabad between the English and the Indians?
4. What was the law of the river and how did it affect the life and death of the Mugger?

Which of the popular sayings below could be used to describe this story?

- Actions speak louder than words
- You get what you deserve in the end
- An eye for an eye, a tooth for a tooth
- Two wrongs do not make a right
- Don't bite the hand that feeds you
- All good things come to he who waits

7. Letting in the Jungle

Understanding the text.
1. How did Mowgli get Hathi to destroy the village?
2. Why did Mowgli want to destroy it?
3. Do you think he had good reason to do so?

Word-building. In this story the wolves and Bagheera sang to each other. Wolves normally howl. Connect the animals below with the sounds they make

Animals			Sound	
dog	cat	mouse	squeak	roar
monkey	lion		hiss	bark
cow	pig	bee	moo	chatter buzz
snake			miaow	grunt

8. The Spring Running

Understanding the text.
1. How did the arrival of Spring affect the plants and animals?
2. How did we know that Mowgli was not as happy as he has been before about Spring?
3. What feelings do you think made Mowgli's stomach seem heavy?
4. What happened when he saw a girl in the village?
5. Do you think Mowgli will be happy in the village? What will he be doing when he is 25?